Steven Kelly was born in 1965. He studied at Warwick and in Vienna and now lives in London.

Steven Kelly

Invisible Architecture

published by Pan Books

First published 1991 in Picador by
Pan Books Ltd Cavaye Place, London SW10 9PG

9 8 7 6 5 4 3 2 1

© Steven Kelly 1991

The right of Steven Kelly to be
identified as the author of this
work has been asserted by him
in accordance with the Copyright,
Designs and Patents Act 1988

ISBN 0 330 31694 X

Photypeset by Input Typesetting Ltd, London

Printed and bound in Great Britain by Billing & Sons Ltd, Worcester for Carol

Acknowledgements

For their friendship, support and encouragement, I should like to thank the following: Martin, Oktay, Ludwig, Eva, Sibylle and Lisi in Vienna; Jo, Karen, Geoff and Gráinne in London.
Special thanks to my family, to my agent, Tony Peake, and my editor at Picador, Martin Fletcher.

Contents

*It is
a ritual*

It is a ritual. The whole thing. I do not see anything bad in that. These are casual affairs but they are also inherently formal. The ritual is the cornerstone of that formality.

I get out of bed, at about nine, and dress. I make myself a coffee – always espresso and preferably Splendid which I have an Italian friend post to me each month. I go to the newsagent and buy a newspaper which I scan for any articles of interest and read the television pages even though I do not have a set. I smoke a couple of cigarettes – Camel, always – and then I will make another coffee. The second coffee of the day kicks my mind into gear and I am ready. So I take my menu notebook – it is the red one – and my fountain pen from the kitchen bookshelf.

I plan the menu very carefully indeed, confident that I will find what I need. If I have to cross the city I will obtain the most esoteric of ingredients. The red notebook is for me to jot down my ideas for the meal and is filled with scrawl and crossings out.

I usually plan the main course first. There is less temptation to complicate things, so it is easier. But when I feel like doing something special, like tonight, when I want to make an effort, I decide on a starter first. From there I select themes, leitmotifs, allow the meal to develop at its own pace, organically perhaps, or like music, like a symphony of colours, smells, shapes and tastes, textures, sounds.

There is nothing wrong with using tinned food on occasions like this. So for a starter I decided to buy some stuffed vine leaves. These I will serve on a platter with some sharp tasting feta cheese, some strong calamata olives, ripe beefsteak tomatoes and freshly baked baguettes. The calamata olives will echo the sweet Spanish green olives, pitted but not stuffed, which I will serve with extra-dry Martinis as an aperitif. And for the main course I will wrap jackets of vine leaves around fresh river trout, bake the fish in a sauce of wine and herbs and serve with baby sweetcorn and broccoli and a butter sauce. But the theme is not simply olives or vine leaves: it is ambiguity, duality, polarity. Just as the stuffed vine leaves combine the piquant taste of the vines and the delicate, bland taste of the rice and onion, so too the sweet, innocuous trout flesh will be offset by the strongly seasoned sauce; an assault on the senses of the best possible type.

And it is a statement, too. My guests tonight are artists and poets, philosophers and critics. I must impress upon them my own understanding of the flavour of life itself, its contradictions, its bitter-sweetness, its ecstatic melancholy. My desperately dry Martinis, made after the model of Buñuel whose recipe still brings me to tears, will jerk my guests into an awareness of their surroundings which will be like a marinade for the evening. And that starter, with its profound intricacies, will demand the attention of their senses, focusing their minds on the meal, giving me the initiative, giving me the power. And when, with my kitchen scissors, I snip open those vine leaf jackets and their anticipation reaches its climax, then I will have them at my feet, cast there by the very force of my imagination and daring.

For dessert, again, something simple yet spectacular. Something to catch them out when they imagine that they have endured the final flames of my desire: chunks of fresh pineapple, ripe nectarines, oranges, lemons, mangoes, cherries, strawberries: I will soak these in Cointreau for several hours and, upon serving, will quickly – before they have a chance to understand my actions – douse them with rum and flambé them at the table. As a kindness to my friends they may take cream. And cheeses and port and coffee. And a spirit of my choice.

Then the evening will be theirs.

When I have planned the menu I write out a list of all the things I will need, ticking off what I already have. I write the list out twice. Once in my green recipe book and once on a sheet of paper which I will take with me to the shops and Naschmarkt. One bottle dry Martini, one bottle Gordon's, a quarter of pitted green olives (Spanish), two tins stuffed vine leaves, half a kilo of feta, two beefsteak tomatoes, a quarter of calamata, six baguettes, a lettuce, herbs for the dressing, four river trout, vine leaves, a bottle of dry white wine, garlic and herbs, unsalted butter, cherry tomatoes, sweetcorn, broccoli . . . This list covers two pages and finishes: two bottles of tequila, lemons, one carton Camel.

Choosing wine to go with the meal is easy. I drink so much of the Tollo Montepulciano d'Abruzzo that some friends call it the 'house' wine. It is a full-bodied Italian red and quite spicy. That the main course is fish does not bother me because it is all part of the statement that I wish to make. Should I buy some other drinks? I decided not to this time because I intended to govern the course of the evening. To a point, at least. I intended to enthuse about each of my choices, so disarming my guests of any they might prefer to make. There was, in any case, whisky and vodka in the cupboard besides the rum, Cointreau, Martini, gin, tequila, port and wine I planned to use.

Once my list is complete, the menu is set. The list becomes an immutable dictate, one to which I subject myself as I shop with an iron discipline. I know that were I to digress from it in any way, were I to act upon any spurious impulse, the meal which I have created mentally in those few perfect moments after that second cup of coffee would cease to be mine. Would belong, somehow, to the city, to the streets, to the shops I enter and the people I meet. This control I have learnt as a result of too many failures and tonight, this night, must be perfect. The perfect ritual to accompany the flawless formal event.

5

Often on Saturday, if I do not have guests coming in the evening, I will sit by the windows overlooking the street and watch the shoppers go by, perhaps listening to some music or drinking some beers. They look so sad, as they fulfil their weekly duties, exploited as consumers just as they are exploited as workers the rest of the week. I try to shop early, usually, to find the best, freshest food and before the market becomes very busy. It closes, anyway, at one as do all the shops here. Then only the flea market is open and sometimes I join my friends there in the afternoon, looking for bargains or spare parts for machines which have broken down, dodging the tramps and the drug addicts who come there to buy or sell.

First I went to the market to buy what I could. It is large and well-stocked, though busy, and they had nearly everything I needed. I met some people I knew there and we went for a beer together. I had to go to the fishmonger to get the trout. It is the only fish shop I know of where the owner will not sell farmed fish. Of course it is more expensive. Nearly three times as much. But I think it is worth it. The calamata I decided to buy from the Cypriot shop on the corner of my street, by the underground station, because I know the owner well and like to do business with him. The fruit I bought from the greengrocer's next to that because it is of a better quality than one finds in the market. The supermarket had the tequila and I asked them to deliver the wine. I ordered two cases for good measure. It would save them some work and they give me a discount.

My guests will bring wine tonight, but I shall take it at the door and put it in the cupboard in the hallway. To take with me to other parties. Other meals.

When I have shopped, when I am home again, I take out my day book. This is a display file and I have over fifty of them, all full, already. In them I keep sheets of paper giving the exact recipe for each dish of the meal and the precise sequence for my preparations. The clear plastic protects the papers from accidental spills as I work so I can use the recipes, if they are good ones, again some time. My Italian friend, who posts me coffee, is proud of his collection of stained cookery books, but he does not need to read the recipes as I do. The file entry for today is quite simple. It should be a relaxing afternoon and early evening to prepare this meal. Sometimes it is not.

I do not write everything in the file. When, for example, I write 'Clean fish' at the beginning, I am writing this for my own information. I do not need to explain to myself the specific procedures which I follow when cleaning fish. I firstly sharpen my fish knife – a gift from one of my guests tonight – and begin to gut the fish. I draw the blade from the anus to the gills, the length of the gut, and pull out the intestines which I throw away. I slice across the underside of the fish, below the gills, to make sure I remove all of the intestines and blood. Then I take my kitchen scissors and snip off the fins and gills. And finally I use a blunt knife to scrape away the scales from the skins. I pat the fish dry and put it in the fridge.

You can tell if a pineapple is ripe by tugging gently at the leaves in the centre at the top. If they come away easily then the pineapple is ripe. I cut it into thick rings, removed the core and sliced away the peel before chopping it into large, uneven chunks. The lemons and oranges I peeled with a knife before chopping roughly. Same with the nectarines and the mango fruits. The cherries I used whole, and the raspberries. The strawberries I simply halved. On a shallow dish I spread the fruit in a single layer, poured over an eighth of a litre of Cointreau and placed the lot in the refrigerator. Done simply, done well.

One of the first things I learnt as a child from my father was the preparation of a salad dressing. He would sit, alone, in his study whilst my mother and my little sister cooked in the kitchen, I watching everything with detached fascination, trying to unravel the secrets of what they were doing. And when the meal was nearly ready my mother would send me to fetch father to make the dressing. His speciality. Every time, I think, it was slightly different. Sometimes he would soak tarragon in white wine vinegar and use this as the base. On other occasions he would use whole-grain mustard and a little thyme. On others he would use only olive oil and vinegar, salt and a little black pepper.

To dress stuffed vine leaves it is essential to get the balance of acidity correct. It is particularly important not to use too much vinegar, though a little too much lemon juice does not matter. In a bowl I mixed nine tablespoons of extra-virgin olive oil with two tablespoons of white wine vinegar and the juice of one lemon. I added a little salt and pepper but no herbs yet.

Then I mixed together, in equal proportions, dried basil, dried thyme and dried oregano. This was for the fish. And I sliced four cloves of garlic and selected four large bay leaves. These I set aside for a while. It was early yet, only five, so it was time to bathe and shave and dress.

My guests tonight were very close friends of mine. My best friends, I suppose they would be called. They were people I wished to impress, to cater for properly. I wanted them to notice that I too had a creative, artistic talent for which they could admire and respect me. I wanted them to know that they had no monopoly on poetry, philosophy, taste.

Cruise – not his real name, of course – comes from Yugoslavia. I call him Cruise, here, because this is the name which Leppard uses for him. Leppard – also not a real name – is from London. He first came to Vienna many years ago and settled here soon after. His German, like that of Cruise, is terrible and to earn his money as an arts critic he has to employ someone to translate his articles. He says that, anyway, he would rather pay the translator than the tax office and it is a question of one or the other. He is a novelist as well, but has never been published. In his latest novel, which I have read, there are three central characters: Cruise, Leppard and Axel. All three are my guests tonight.

Axel is from Denmark. His German is fluent, with just a trace of an accent. In Leppard's novel, Axel is an aristocratic German whose art is life itself but who is always getting into trouble. This says a good deal about Leppard's perception of his friends because, although he is from a wealthy background, Axel is hard working, down to earth and seldom in any trouble. In the novel Leppard is an account handler for an advertising company in London. This does not reflect any desire on the real Leppard's part. Rather it is his acknowledgement that as a critic and an aspiring novelist, much of his energy is expended on 'keeping his clients sweet'. He hates it. Cruise, too, is mythologized. In reality he is a brilliant poet, a talented philosopher, a good friend to his friends. In the novel he becomes a black 'speed-freak' from Amsterdam whose philosophy is derived from the streets, who can never hold down a job, who 'cruises' through life. It could not be further from the truth. Leppard's novel is not very good because, I suspect, he is too close to his characters, or at least to the people upon whom the characters are based. Yet for all that there is insight enough for me to feel comfortable thinking of them now by the names Leppard has given them. There are certain truths in his representation which are important to me and which meant that I enjoyed his novel, good or bad.

I try to take a bath if I have people coming to supper. The hour I spend washing myself is another part of the ritual. It ensures that my passions do not flow too quickly, gives me time to reflect upon the progress of the preparations thus far. There is a Chinese saying to the effect that he who can tell how an oak tree unfolds from an acorn can predict the course of the future. I examine my acorns, follow through the numerous conceivable unfoldings which are to take place during the evening. Tonight is to be special. It must be mapped out in meticulous detail. I can only provide parameters for the action of the story, but they must be considered well. I wish, perhaps, to challenge their conceit tonight and to do this a certain stature is required.

Cruise came to Vienna because of politics and he lives here still for them. In Yugoslavia, when he was younger, there was little scope for a philosopher of his calibre to speak his mind. His socialist beliefs were, perhaps, a little too ideologically pure for his less committed compatriots. He travelled firstly: to Turkey where he was caught up in the communist underground; to Italy where he was an activist and had friends in the Italian Red Army Faction – he was arrested there twice, though never convicted; and to Holland where he lived with anarchist squatters, helping to run a community centre in the city. In many ways I think he is here to rest, or even retire. He is still active but with his work in the restaurant near here he has little time and he is, after all, older than any of us. He does not write so much now. One poem a year or so, he told me recently. And occasionally he contributes to magazines here and abroad. He takes an innocent pleasure in seeing his name in print and walks around with the publication in which it has appeared, showing it to everyone he meets. 'This is me.' But he lives here illegally and the strain of that is all too apparent. I bought him a false passport for 40,000 schillings which helps, but not enough. He lives now more for his friendships and has mellowed slightly with age. Or perhaps he is coming to the knowledge that an abstract love for humanity cannot replace a real love of people. I have asked him that before and he has never answered but I think it may be true. I envy him his experience of life, I who have lived in this city, in this apartment by the Naschmarkt, all of my life. I have only travelled twice, to Prague and Venice, and have ski'd in the Alps a few times. But that was with my family. I have not left the city for ten years now. And have not worked for twelve. There is money enough. I see no point in working for the sake of it and I prefer to cook, to entertain.

Cruise never talks much about his politics with me. I think he suspects that I have little sympathy for his type of socialism. I thought that Kreisky was a great man in many respects, though I would go no further than that. Indeed, I think that Cruise suspects me of many things which are anathema to him. Leppard is on another plane when it comes to politics. He is a romantic anarchist on the lines of Shelley. He believes all government and authority to be wrong and tells us that love is the true revolution – though he is no hippy. Needless to say, I do not agree. But his views are at least entertaining where Cruise's are clinical and morose. I do find politics interesting, however, and I admire the way these three, with their so different beliefs, remain friends. Axel's views are closest to my own. Sometimes we see each other without the other two and stay up late into the night talking about the disintegration of values, the need for strong moral authority and governments free from corruption. At the same time, were I to say anything against the views held by Leppard or Cruise, Axel would take it to be a personal insult. Such is their loyalty.

When I was shaving the telephone rang. I did not answer it but Leppard left a message which I could hear from the bathroom. They would be coming early. At seven-thirty instead of eight. They wanted to go dancing at midnight. I do not deny that I was annoyed, though I should not have been. Perhaps I was more annoyed with myself for not anticipating this possibility – it has happened before. I suppose I felt that this evening was so important to me that they would not dream of upsetting my plans in so simple a way. But every time I invite them to dinner it is important to me in the way that it is tonight. This evening is nothing special, there will be other evenings like it again and again. There have been many before.

Not to worry. I still had sufficient time for my preparations and, perhaps, the promise of endless drink would keep them here. My naïvety depresses me at times. It was just after six so I quickly dried my hair and returned to the kitchen. I sliced the beefsteak tomatoes, chopped the feta into neat cubes, arranged the stuffed vine leaves, tomato, cheese and calamata on a bed of lettuce on a platter. I sprinkled some dried oregano and some fresh basil over this and poured on half of the dressing. The rest I would use another time. I put the platter in the fridge and took out the four trout. These I seasoned inside and out with sea salt, freshly ground black pepper and the mix of herbs which I had previously prepared. Inside each fish, in the stomach cavity, I placed one bay leaf and a few slices of garlic. I put the fish into a dish and sprinkled it with a little lemon juice. Then I put it back into the fridge to soak up the marinade for a while. After this I broke up the broccoli and put it into a pan of slightly salted cold water. I sliced up some of the cherry tomatoes I had bought and, the bulk of the preparation done, opened four bottles of wine and poured myself a glass.

Now it was time to prepare the vine leaves with which I would wrap the fish. This I did, simply, by pouring boiling water over them and allowing them to stand for twenty minutes. This makes them tender, though I do not intend that my guests should eat them. Rather their purpose is to add flavour to the trout flesh and also, when peeled from the fish, they will bring away the skin which has a pleasing cosmetic effect, I feel. I set the table with place mats, cutlery, side plates, napkins and glasses. No extra seasonings, however. Half of the unsalted butter I curled into attractive knobs and put into a butter dish. This will not be a very healthy meal, I am afraid. When the vine leaves were ready I took out the trout and wrapped each one in an overcoat of three leaves. Then I drizzled a little olive oil onto the baking dish, sprinkled on some more herbs and seasonings, put down a layer of baby sweetcorn over this, placed the trout upon the sweetcorn and seasoned again. And I placed a layer of tomato slices over the trout in vine leaves to keep the overcoat moist on top. Finally I poured half a bottle of Muscadet into the dish and the doorbell rang.

'Cruise, welcome, are you alone?'

'The others will come together.'

He had not brought any wine with him. I was made cautious by this and the fact that he had come first, alone. It meant I would have to wait for the others before serving the Martinis. I wanted to tell them all of Buñuel's recipe at the same time. But I could not leave him without a drink.

'We owe you lots of meals now.'

'Not to worry, Cruise, you know I enjoy your visits.'

We walked through to the dining room and, just as Cruise sat down and I was about to offer him something, the doorbell rang again. I would be able to tell my story.

'Have you heard of Buñuel's recipe for a dry Martini?'

Cruise smiled and nodded. I motioned to him to tell it himself, but he insisted that I complete my anecdote.

'You take a Martini glass, like this.' I held a glass up in the air. 'How is it? You pour in two fingers of gin.' I did so. 'And you take a bottle of vermouth. Noilly Prat is suggested by Buñuel. You hold the bottle up so that a shaft of light passes through the bottle and shines onto the glass of gin for just a few instants, add ice and an olive and . . .'

Leppard and Axel started to laugh and immediately followed suit, pouring gin into their glasses, holding the Martini bottle up to the light and sipping the surrealist cocktail of gin and more gin. Cruise poured himself a glass of Martini, held the gin bottle to the light for a moment and drank the drink down straight with ice but no olive. Leppard and Axel laughed again and so did I. My opening scene had gone well.

Leppard's character in his novel is that of a predatory male who is apparently of an infinite capacity to convince attractive women of his integrity and sincerity. The lesson, that a leopard cannot change its spots, is learnt the hard way by a succession of women until he meets Marie. Marie learns the truth: Leppard's first and only love deserted him and that predatory 'instinct' is actually the desperate search of a vulnerable and sensitive man for someone to take away the pain. By learning this and showing Leppard that she appreciates his sensitivity and vulnerability, Marie becomes Leppard's second true love. The scene is set for a happy ending until we learn that Marie's best friend killed herself after being left by Leppard and Marie was out for revenge. Having gained his trust she leaves him. To all appearances he is a broken man and spends much time drunk. Then, one day his friend Cruise tells him: 'You gotta cruise, man,' and he does. The story ends with the three heroes leaving London in search of other hunting grounds 'where the girls are prettier and the pubs open late'.

Leppard does write out of desire, wish fulfilment in this respect. He has never really loved anyone and never will. But he feels that he should. Unwilling to act out that role in real life, he consigns it to paper. It makes for artificial contradictions between the man and his writing which are utterly see-through. Yet that in itself provides other, deeper contradictions which are fascinating where the artificial ones are not.

After two or three Martinis I invited my guests to sit at the table – we had been standing, strangely. I served them the starter. As I was putting the platter of stuffed vine leaves and cheese and calamata and tomatoes on the table, I realized I had not cut the bread. So I went back to the kitchen to get it ready. I waited in the kitchen for a few moments, quietly listening to the voices of the others. I think I felt a little worried, as if something were not quite right, but I put it down to nerves. I do not believe in destiny.

They are all intimidated by formality. In some way at least. And they all react to it completely differently. I generally feel threatened, rather, by Cruise when I am with him, because I suppose that I feel him looking right inside me or chewing me over like a cow with its cud. But the moment I present him with something which he perceives to be of a very high quality, he falls silent. Often, on birthdays or at Christmas or New Year I have opened a bottle of good champagne to share with my friends and he has not said one word until the last drops from the bottle were drunk. I chose the starter tonight partly because it has a Balkan flavour to it, I think. But still, from the moment it was served to the last mouthful of the main course, he was virtually silent. Of course it could be that he simply wishes to appreciate the food with which he is served. To appreciate sensual things fully, one has to be very quiet and Cruise is the sort of person who would realize that. He withdraws into a private universe, one which meets the common world at a tangent, and allows events and lives to pass him by. As well as this, though, it is true that he is unused to the dictates of others and resents them. He is by nature a leader. I have been to parties and meals at his place and he talks constantly from the moment his guests arrive. He can be quite the finest raconteur when it suits him, though this is still strange to me having seen him and his silence so often. It is the formality which does this. The conscious existence of self in an alien, rigorously structured environment. He is the only one of the three who does realize that the situation is a formal one. The subtitle of his doctorate was, after all, 'On The Poem as an Aesthetic Object'. It is not surprising that Cruise, of all people, should have some insight into form and its relationship to content.

Leppard is unused to form. Or, at least, he is used to form when it is something he can observe, something he can relate to as a spectator, commenting upon it, remaining at all times a few steps removed from it. Interestingly, his reviews and essays deal with form frequently. Intellectually, academically, he has a good understanding of the way in which form should – or can – match content. But that objective view upon which he prides himself is never applied to his own surroundings with the same stringency. He never acknowledges, in his criticisms, that the spectator or the reader is a party to the form of the art, a party to the formality of reading or watching. So, for him, a social gathering, something in which he, the critic, participates, is a formless, fluid thing. Where anything can happen. When we go out, the four of us, he is usually the one who decides where we should go next, what we should do. Now to Tunnel in the eighth, now Europa in the seventh or to a disco in the 'Bermuda Triangle', the tourist trap in the centre of the city where there are always girls and free drinks. Leppard is an unwitting dictator. He fails to notice that, when a dinner guest, the initiative is no longer his own. Still he attempts to control the course of the conversation or the speed at which events – events I am now staging – will take place. The rest of us had started our meal, but he had just lit another cigarette and we felt uncomfortable, eating in the presence of this observer. He is a master of his trade.

Axel, though, is the perfect dinner guest. He responds to questions, initiates conversation with practised ease. He does have a certain aristocratic quality in this respect. He knows what to say and when. He never compliments me on my cooking. He knows that to do so would be to suggest that it might conceivably be anything less than the best for my guests. Leppard, with his lower-class background, praises every mouthful loudly and without feeling. Cruise says: 'Thank you, my friend, may your hands be blessed.' As if I have done his stomach a favour rather than his taste buds – and taste – an honour. Axel, too, is intimidated in his own way. This shows in his behaviour when he is drunk. When it is late and we are in a bar or restaurant, his aristocratic sense of proper behaviour gives way to an aristocratic desire for debauchery and amusement. He understands form and appears comfortable with it. But he needs to escape it often. I do not like to see him at these times. He is not himself.

The starter worked. Although, actually, insubstantial, my guests felt quite full at the end of it, they said. In any case, I only switched on the oven now so there would be a fair interval – of fifty minutes or so – before the main course was served. We talked about what we had been doing. Nothing unusual, it seemed. Axel had a new contract – he is never short of them. He is an interior designer and makes the furniture he designs specially for each place he works on. He is a brilliant architect. I had him redesign the interior of this apartment a couple of years ago and I love what he has done. He is a different person when he works. Like me when I cook, and Cruise when he is writing a poem, I imagine. He throws himself into his work, becomes absorbed by what he is doing, a part of the project. His understanding of materials, of textures and of finishes, of colour and light makes me feel like a blind man in a gallery. When we were working on this place I would give him my ideas – crude outlines at best. From his understanding of his work, partly, but also from his understanding of me he would interpret those notions and within hours could produce detailed sketches which seemed, in comparison to my faint suggestions, like Platonic ideals brought to earth, retrieved by the master craftsman from their cave.

The flat is a Jugendstil showcase, combining the very best of the functionality of Loos and the decorative brilliance of Olbrich and Wagner. There are prints of paintings by Klimt, Schiele and Kokoschka in every room. And the centrepiece of the entire apartment is a Hundertwasser which I bought at Axel's suggestion and great expense and which every guest admires. I adore Hundertwasser's work. It captures the very best of Viennese art and the modern Austrian spirit. My only regret about this place is that my parents could not have seen what has been done. Though my father considered the Secession painters and architects to be decadent and would have despised the Hundertwasser, my mother would have appreciated the change. In all the years that they lived here, the apartment was never redecorated and the only change was in the quantity of ornaments and kitsch decorations which gathered here in ever greater amounts. When I was very young I bought a book about the German expressionist painter Otto Dix, whose work I like no longer but whom I continue to find fascinating. My father destroyed the book in a fit of fury, saying that Dix was an obscenity, that he wished to corrupt the morals of the young and spread mental illness and syphilis.

'Cruise, did you go to the Hundertwasserhaus yet?'

'I went only last week. I bought a book there. Of his paintings and his writings. It is very interesting, but he is a confused philosopher. There is little sense in his statements.'

'How do you mean?'

'For example, in his speech "On False Art" he says that "if an artist refuses to destroy, he is spat upon by this strange Mafia of the arts" and yet, in the previous sentence, he claims that the artist who seeks "the true values" is considered a backward reactionary. But I would argue . . .'

At this point Cruise started to wag his right forefinger in the air in front of Leppard's nose. Leppard bit it playfully. Cruise turned to him, staring slightly, and slapped him quite hard on the back of the head. Leppard giggled, but was subdued for some time afterwards.

'. . . I would argue that in order to find "true values" we must tear apart the past, discover in what it is that the art of the past consists, and reconstruct our world from there. The process of art is one of reincorporating that which we see and discover from our pasts, from our cultures, from our everyday experiences of the present into our modern constructions. But to discover, we must first undo.'

'But is he not saying precisely that we should first accept the constructions of the past for their beauty and for what they tell us directly and secondly create beauty from the world in which we live to match that beauty of the past. For example, he says in that same essay: "Why don't you ask your grandmother what is good and beautiful. The absence of kitsch makes our life unbearable. Without the romantic spirit nothing works." '

'And then he says: "We have lost the sense of beauty." Does he have to be both right and wrong in only one essay?'

'I like him, nevertheless.'

'I like his paintings.'

'What have you been doing, anyway?'

Leppard. He hates confrontation, even on a certain philosophical or rhetorical level. Neither Cruise nor myself cared. Cruise is the sort of person Hundertwasser had in mind when he wrote that essay. Someone whose 'genius' lies in his ability to rip to shreds the human soul and call it detritus or call the act of doing so art. They are perfect poems in terms of their use of language, their structure, their internal dynamics. But they hold nothing for the future, nothing for the man or woman on the street. Not for me, at least. We retired from the duel willingly.

'I have not been doing a great deal, really. Reading, writing letters, going to the opera or the theatre. Sometimes a film. I met my astrologer friend for lunch, yesterday it was. He is very depressed at the moment. And bored of writing horoscopes. He seems to find it an immense strain, having all those people depending upon him for their happiness or titillation every day and his wife has left him, now. She just walked out one day and he thinks, perhaps, that he will kill himself. I do not know if he will, though. Again, he has his responsibilities to his readers and is too good a man to let them down. There are enough suicides in this city, anyway.'

'I'm sick of my work. It's getting boring. I've been taking in at least one book and one film every day for the last fortnight, now. It's ridiculous. Perhaps you should meet my editor. I think you could do the job well.'

'I am not a critic. Why do you not do something completely different. Give up the arts altogether and become a postman.'

'Yes, why don't you, Leppard. You would make a good worker.'

'Easy for you to say, my friend. You don't need to work for your living. And for you Cruise. You happily spend your life bumming drinks from your mates so that they have to work much harder than they would.'

'What are friends for? You happily have more money than you need and you don't have the intellectual calibre not to work. You would get bored, you are so simple.'

'Get lost, Cruise, you wouldn't know a free lunch if it landed on your lap.'

'The food should be ready in five minutes or so.'

I took the fish out of the oven and drained off the juices into a dish. I put the trout back into the oven to finish cooking and strained the juices into another pan. I reduced them down until there were only about four tablespoons of liquid remaining. Then I added knobs of unsalted butter one at a time, whisking vigorously as I did so until the sauce was creamy and thick. Then I served the trout on plates with the vegetables. I put the plates before my guests and snipped open the jackets with my kitchen scissors and finally poured a little of the butter sauce over each fish. For once even Leppard was captured by the events taking place before him on the table.

Cruise has been in trouble with the police again. Foolishly he continues to go on demonstrations against this issue or that one, for this cause or another. Or course the police film the demonstrators and, in Vienna, it is not difficult to put a name to most faces eventually. So they raided his house last week and he was lucky that his Austrian neighbours are communists. He rang them when he heard the police in the street and escaped through the roof of his apartment. They opened the skylight in their attic and allowed him to come inside until the police had gone. He has moved to another friend's house for the moment. I offered him a room here, of course, but he does not want to put me at any risk when it is not essential. I am relieved, slightly, though the implicit insult does not go unnoticed either by myself or the other two. He knows that my greatest fear is of getting into trouble with the police. Not of breaking the law, but of being found out. The shame would cause me much pain. When I bought him his passport – that is, when I gave him the money to buy it – I was terrified that the cash might be traced to me in some way.

'This is great. You've excelled yourself, my man. Really good. Think I'll mention this in my column on Tuesday. Where did you get the recipe?'

'You must excuse our friend. He comes from a strange land over the sea where it is simply not done to be creative in the kitchen and where bad manners are considered *de rigueur* rather than simply amusing, as we find them in my country.'

'*Naff off Axel, you slimy git, it was a bleeding joke*, all right.'

'They also speak in a bizarre tongue unknown outside their land.'

'And you, Cruise, you apeman.'

The phone rang, so I answered it and the others fell silent.

'It is for you, Cruise. I do not know who it is.'

He took the phone into the sitting room next door and spoke quickly and quietly for a few minutes. The rest of us did not speak, concentrating on peeling the delicate trout flesh from the bones, savouring the flavours as they came.

By the time Cruise had finished on the phone – he made a couple of calls as well – the rest of us had finished eating.

'Trouble?'

But he did not answer immediately. He sat at his place and tucked his napkin under his chin, into the top of his black polo neck sweater – he is so very much the existentialist intellectual-worker at times – and ate his food in silence whilst I described the ingredients to Leppard. Half-way through the description I was giving, Leppard held up both of his hands, palms facing me.

'Enough, enough. You lost me ages ago, my man. I guess we'd all better leave the cooking to you. Don't want a job, do you? Could do my ironing while you're at it.'

'Our friend is a philistine. You know, I took him to Stockholm for a week a while ago – you remember. We had a smörgsbord. This guy asked me to tell the waiter the fish was undercooked and he'd rather have it hot anyway.'

'This man is a party animal. Food is for eating and broken hearts are for assholes. Frankie Zappa said that, don't you know?'

'You're slipping into character again, *Leppard*.'

Even Cruise laughed now.

'So what's the currency, Cruise? They busted you again?'

'Just some friends. I may have to leave early. They will call again.'

'That is OK, Cruise, though there is a long way to go.'

'That's what we want to hear, my man. More food, more drink, then slip out into the night . . .'

'Perhaps not too soon. My friends never hurry if they can help it.'

When everyone had finished eating I cleared the table and loaded the dishwasher, but I did not turn it on. They would not feel like eating the dessert yet but I poured some cream into a jug and drained off the Cointreau from the fruit. This I would use as the base for a punch or perhaps a special sauce on another occasion. I put the fruit into a serving dish. And I opened two more bottles of wine. I did not think that we would drink it but it was better to be on the safe side. I have heard some people say that perhaps it is not necessary to allow red wine to breathe. I continue to do so anyway. It is another part of the ritual.

In the dining room my guests were talking very quietly. So that I could not hear, I imagined. Probably Cruise was telling Leppard about the phone call. They deliberately do not participate in each other's adventures, on the whole. But Leppard and Cruise, in particular, conspire constantly. At the various newspapers and radio stations where Leppard works there is a lot of in-fighting. In the beginning it was easy for Leppard to make advances. He had a brawling, street-fighting style which took my mild-mannered compatriots by surprise. They have learnt from him, however, and the in-fighting which goes on is vicious. He deals with the tactics of this himself, but Cruise is the master strategist and guides him all the way. By the same token it is Leppard who advises Cruise on the next move he should make in order to achieve his longer-term plans. Leppard understands people better than any of us – at least he understands adversaries. Whilst Leppard is the protégé of Cruise, he is also his principal equerry. They never involve me in these discussions. Usually I am left with Axel whilst the others 'go for a walk' to talk things through. I do not see why it has to be this way, though I suspect that it is Cruise who dictates that it shall be so. Leppard has never objected to playing before an audience and relates the details of every development to me anyway.

'Ready for some dessert?'

I put the bowls on the table and, in the kitchen, poured some dark rum over the fruit. I carried the dish through to the dining room and swiftly lit it with my lighter. The effect was good as the bluish flame flared and then subsided.

'Woah! We're being treated tonight, my man.'

Leppard affects a turn of phrase which he imagines to be intimate and friendly but which, in fact, is inane at the best of times. The banality of some of his comments tonight offended me. I think Axel was embarrassed by them as well. Though he is too polite to even hint at that, and possibly even too loyal to admit the feeling to himself anyway. Cruise stares at Leppard blankly when he makes these comments. His lack of response denotes his position in the group as its mature and calm leader. He occasionally remonstrates with the other two if they do things in public which embarrass him. There was a time in a bar when we were together. One of the cool bars in the seventh. We ate a salad with olives and Leppard and Axel started to throw olive pits at some of the other customers. They did it very cleverly so that none of their victims could identify the culprits and it was quite amusing to see them staring around the room looking at everyone. I remember edging my chair away from the table at which we were sitting in a half-hearted attempt to dissociate myself from the group. Cruise excused himself to me before talking to them rapidly in English which I have difficulty in following. It is one of the only times that the three of them have talked in English in front of me. They are very considerate in that respect. It is the only time I have ever seen them argue as they did then. Leppard stormed out of the bar but Axel remained behind. Cruise then lectured him, and me, at great length about maturity and being sensitive to the feelings of others. Leppard soon returned and the argument was forgotten. Later that same evening, going home along the Zieglergasse where the bar in which we had been is at one end, all three started to walk over the cars parked bumper to bumper the length of the street. I slowed my pace until they might appear, to an observer, to be none of my friends.

It is when they do things like this that I feel most distant from them. They revel in their unconventionality and cynicism. When they are drunk, at least. There was the time here, in my apartment, when we were sitting on the window ledges in the dining and sitting rooms which overlook the street. Opposite the building was a bar where skinheads met. Youngsters mostly who should not be out drinking. On this occasion three skinheads, two boys and a girl, saw us looking from the window as they were leaving the bar. They shouted something which I did not hear and Cruise shouted back 'Fuck off Nazis' – in English. One of them called to us to come down and fight. We did not, of course, but spoke to him in English. He did not understand, although he was wearing a T-shirt with a British flag on the back and a picture of a bulldog on the front. Eventually he picked up two large stones from the side of the road. Cruise ran to the kitchen and brought empty bottles for us to throw. As soon as the first stone was thrown, which came straight through an open window but did no damage, we threw the empty bottles at the skinheads who ran away. I was worried that they would return one day, when the others were not here. They did not, though, and the bar has closed down now. Cruise asked me if I had thrown a bottle and seemed not to believe me when I told him that I had.

None of us managed to finish our desserts. I decided not to serve the cheese and biscuits and offered them coffee and port which they accepted instantly, with glee almost. When I had finished serving this, Leppard asked us if we would like to smoke some hashish. I do not care about it. I have had it, of course, but it made me feel nauseous and stupid. And I would not enjoy, especially, to smoke it with these friends. Their closeness is such, anyway, that I feel like a voyeur upon their intimacies. Fortunately Axel knows this, and Cruise seldom takes the drug – it would be an unnecessary risk – so Leppard put away his papers and the little box which he carries with him everywhere. The port was very good and Axel said so, unusually for him.

'Well, my man, you've done us proud tonight. Never knew you Austrians could be so spot on when it came to food.'

'Leppard's main experience of Austrian food is the McDonalds on the Mariahilferstrasse. He still thinks Wienerschnitzel is a type of sausage.'

'Get lost, Axel, at least we don't eat raw fish in England.'

'Do you have a cigarette for me, my friend?'

I went to the kitchen to get a packet of Camel for Cruise. As a joke I placed it on a silver tray – one stolen by Leppard from a coffee house once, in fact. Next to it I put a book of matches and took the tray through to Cruise. They laughed, then Axel shook his head slowly. 'No, no, not like that, like this.' He took the tray from Cruise's side, just as Cruise was reaching for the packet, and went back into the kitchen. A few seconds later he returned.

'Like this, my brother, this is how you do it.' He had unwrapped the plastic from the cigarette packet and torn open the silver foil at one corner. From the corner some cigarettes were protruding, ready to be taken. And he had folded back the match book and bent one match forward ready to use. He bowed to Cruise and presented him with the tray. 'Comrade.'

Cruise nodded graciously and we all laughed again as he took a cigarette, flipped it high into the air, caught it in his mouth and, in one action, lit it with his Zippo.

'Comrade, my deepest and most sincere thanks for your kindness.'

'Comrade, it is but a duty to serve one's brother as they work in the great struggle against imperialist oppression and world capitalism.'

I find this aspect of their friendship to be unusual. They have a limitless capacity to entertain and amuse themselves with the most trivial things. In others this might suggest trivial minds, but with them it is different. Behind everything is a sense of irony which, though unspoken, provides the real humour of the situations they create so spontaneously. They are aware of the contradictions which infest the world like so many cancerous cells. Profoundly so. They find a dark pleasure in their ability to be so contemptuous of them.

I poured myself some more port and sat back in my chair.

'Shall we sit next door?'

I was pleased that Cruise had suggested this. Had I been the one to say it he, or the others, might have taken it as an opportunity to leave. A natural break in the performance. The end of an act.

Whereas the stark lines of the dining room were designed to focus attention on the dining table, Axel created in the sitting room a general ambience of warmth, comfort and relaxation. The focus of the room is dual: the Hundertwasser, one of the earliest in which his famous spiral features, hangs on the east wall. We decided that the chairs and sofas should be organized in a loose horseshoe, the open end of which is directly below the painting. That large coffee table in the centre, with its dark, highly polished wood, was imported from Italy. Axel said that he thought it would be better than anything he could make. I polish it myself and do not allow the cleaning woman to touch it. The glass-fronted cabinets around the room are very carefully positioned. The effect is such that the painting is reflected or re-reflected and its image can be seen in the surface of the coffee table wherever one sits. The idea of having the furniture in a horseshoe was my idea. It was Axel's genius which achieved the remainder of the effect.

'There was something else, my friend. About the book. The essay entitled "Mouldiness Manifesto Against Rationalism in Architecture". You know it?'

'Yes, the Seckau speech from '58.'

'He claims that the straight line is godless and immoral.'

'Yes.'

'There are straight lines in the building at Löwengasse which I am sure were only achieved through the use of a T-square. Do you not think?'

'I do not know. I do not think it matters. He is proposing a principle, not attempting to enact an ideal. Hundertwasser is a visionary. The world is only now beginning to catch up with his ideas. You would agree that the world is catching up?'

Cruise was silent for a while. Then:

'Do you think the house is beautiful?'

'Yes, do you not?'

'I think it is a work of art.'

'What are you trying to say?'

'Without the T-square, or straight line, his art would be an impossibility. His opposition to its use is not consistent.'

'Why does he have to be consistent? He is an artist.'

'You, I know, consider the Dadaists degenerates. I consider Hundertwasser regressive.'

'What do you think, Axel?'

'Me? I think the house is beautiful. I think the painting is beautiful. And I don't care much about theories – his or Cruise's.'

'Leppard?'

Leppard was standing, his nose only inches from the painting.

'The guy's a head-fucker. No getting away from it.'

Cruise looked at him thoughtfully:

'Yes. A head-fucker. He talks a lot and paints great pictures, but anyway. . .'

'Why do you dislike him, Cruise? It seems to be something personal with you.'

'It is. I don't think Hundertwasser is a Nazi by any means. He's partly Jewish, isn't he? But his aesthetic – it reminds me of the Nazi aesthetic. You know, all those paintings of very maternal women and blond, blue-eyed supermen, all very close to the earth and public-spirited. . . I don't mean that exactly, not the way he paints. But his ideology. In fact it isn't even what Hundertwasser says himself. More what other people see in him that disturbs me. He's turned into a national hero and his, actually very internationalist, green beliefs are turned around into a nationalism which I don't think is good. But if, by designing Austria's postage stamps, he allows himself to be seen in that way, then he is at fault.'

'Anyone can be misinterpreted. You called *Thus Spake Zarathustra* a holy book, once. Remember?'

'The difference being that Nietzsche did not have a foreknowledge of fascism by which to avoid it. I'm not sure about Nietzsche either, really.'

'Cruise, stop giving our host such a hard time.'

I decided it was time to open the tequila bottle so I excused myself and went to the kitchen to get it. I brought lemons and salt as well, and some fresh glasses.

By tacit agreement, Cruise and I did not resume our discussion until we had drunk three shots of tequila each. Axel was obviously quite drunk now. Of the three of them he is the one who is least able to take his drink. He is often ill or passes out. Like the other two, he does not know when to stop. Cruise and I can out-drink the other two on any occasion. And often we do so. After the third tequila Leppard and Axel decided to play chess. The winner, when we play, must buy his opponent dinner at a restaurant of the loser's choice. Anyone suspected of trying to lose on purpose – it has never happened – would be judged the loser of a series. A series is five games so the loser must buy three meals for the winner before the next game is played. At least one game must be played by each possible pairing every month and we try to go to dinner all together. We are very competitive but there is a humility associated with victory, brought on by its expense – sometimes two or three thousand schillings for one game if it has been a good one and the loser has played well. If the loser has played badly, he will nominate the sausage stand at the end of the Naschmarkt as his chosen 'restaurant'.

Cruise picked up my copy of the Hundertwasser book. He leafed through the pages a little, stopped at one, carried on some more, put the book down on the coffee table. Leppard was on white and started with an unusual move which made Axel spend more time on his opening than usual.

'What do you think of his green ideas generally? Would you seriously want to live in a world where every individual was responsible for disposing of their own faeces?'

'I do not say I endorse him fully. The point about the humus toilet is that it is an inevitable necessity for human survival. Not just a hippy's toy. He is right, I think, that we are alienated from our bodily functions.'

'Oh, yes, he certainly is, but that is a Marxist issue, not an aesthetic one.'

'Come on, Cruise, Marx does not have a monopoly on the truth. Not these days.'

'Hundertwasser is crazy if he thinks I want a very close association with my own shit. There are few animals which actually nurture their own excrement.'

'Though the scarab was a sacred creature.'

'Leppard, are you trying to lose this match? Cruise, did you see that?'

Axel knew that Leppard had outwitted him already or he would not have said this. The trap was the same one that Leppard had used on me a few days before and I had fallen into it as well. Cruise knows this so we watched them play the game out now, hoping to learn a little more about Leppard's new move and thus avoid the same fate another time.

'Have you men sorted out the meaning of life yet?'

'Our host wishes to recreate the prelapsarian pastoral ideal.'

'Too damn right, my son. Smash the Machines!'

'I am quite serious, though, Cruise. The use of the humus toilet is just an extension of the principles of organic farming. That makes some sense, surely.'

'I'm no eco-freak, but sure, I think the green movement is important. That's not the issue, my friend. The issue is whether by turning the problem of ecology into an aesthetic one, Hundertwasser is not performing an essentially fascist function – whatever his personal views in that connection. If it is possible to define Hitler's attitude towards the Jews at all, one might say that The Final Solution was an aesthetic one in the purest sense. Obviously, having failed to get into the Vienna Art Academy, we can say that Hitler's taste – and ability – was lacking, but the definition of the Shoah as aesthetic in conception could stand. Aesthetics are not appropriate when it comes to political decisions. They are too subjective.'

'Ignoring the Shoah, one can say that Hitler's aesthetic was shared by many people. Almost the majority.'

'Yes. I went to Mauthausen two weeks ago.'

'I have been there.' I said this very quietly.

'You've been in the Commandant's office? You know about that Dutch guy? The cripple who was admitted to the camp and the Commandant said "I want him *on* my desk tomorrow"?'

'Yes.'

'That's your popular Nazi aesthetic. Please don't try to defend it. They killed many of my relatives in Yugoslavia. My own father died as a result of injuries he sustained during torture. Though he survived ten years, I never met him.'

'You think we Austrians are all still Nazis, do you not, Cruise?'

'No, my friend, but your countrymen were misled – are still being misled – by Hitler and his aesthetic.'

'That would seem to be readily apparent. Do you blame Hundertwasser for the current climate?'

'Not directly, but the issue is always one of freedom versus slavery.'

'I was simply saying – still am – that a world where we are closer to nature is a more beautiful, more inhabitable one.'

'We don't live in a beautiful world, my friend. Not for a long time.'

I poured another round of tequilas.

'OK, Leppard, I concede. But for that one you can take me to that Greek place by the opera.'

'It'll be a pleasure, my man. A sweet pleasure. Now, shall we get on with the serious business?'

Leppard always becomes blasé when he wins. He has the least natural talent and practises for hours, playing his chess computer. The computer teaches him set pieces which he tries out on us from time to time. Sometimes they are transparent and he loses quickly. Occasionally they work and when they do he buys dinner with his Visa gold card.

I decided to put on some music, hoping to lighten the atmosphere. Cruise had receded into silence and was chain-smoking and serving himself three tequilas for every two we drank. Leppard and Axel were joking with me about my music collection. I have only opera or cool jazz and one or two other cassettes given to me but never played. They say I am confused because I listen either to the carefully staged formality of opera or to the free improvisation of the jazz. They do not understand how I can adore both with an equal passion. When I started trying to justify it, I suddenly found it funny as well and laughed too.

Axel was very drunk by this time. He got to his feet and lurched to the door. We heard him vomiting into the toilet a short time later. Leppard laughed loudest, though even he knew that he was next. Axel returned, only slightly embarrassed. It has happened many times before and he knows we do not care. I felt a little hungry, so I offered my guests the cheese and biscuits we had been too full to eat earlier. Cruise declined the offer but the other two said yes. In the kitchen I thought about what Cruise had said. I was a little annoyed with him, but I thought that something might have been bothering him as he is never normally so critical of the Austrian people. Usually he is sympathetic to the situation in which we found ourselves in 1938 and, indeed, in recent times.

Back in the sitting room the others were animated.

'You know, in Denmark we say that you only truly know your friends if you have been drunk with them.'

'We know, Axel, you tell us every time. I do not know why.'

'He thinks it's a reasonable excuse for his disgraceful behaviour. What do you reckon, Cruise?'

Sometimes Cruise has a look in his eye which we all recognize.

It is a distant, almost trancelike expression which always precedes one of his obscure parables.

'There is a story, from Turkey. . .'

We all laughed. It was a running joke with us.

'. . . about a tribe in the East. This tribe was involved in a blood feud with a neighbouring clan which had already caused many deaths and much hardship. One day the chief of the tribe summoned his captains and told them: "Issue a decree to the women of my tribe. Tell them that if any of them should lose a husband or a son or a father or a brother, they must not cry." The captains protested. Why should their chief issue such an order to the women of the tribe? Was not their prerogative that of any wife or mother, daughter or sister – to mourn the passing of their loved ones? "Tell the women of my tribe that if any of them weep when they lose a loved one, they may have their head delivered to me at their convenience on the following day." Again the captains begged their chief to explain or reconsider but he was adamant and the decree was issued. Within weeks the feud was won and the captains asked their chief again about the decree. "Pain must be used, at times of war, to build new strength. Just as muscles are built by hard exercise in peace time. If a woman shall cry she remains weak and in times of war the women too must be strong." '

'Great, Cruise, just great.'

What he meant, I think, was that if Axel wanted to invoke his culture to tell us we were his friends, we should allow him to do so.

'Thank you, Cruise, at least someone around here understands me.'

'Shall we have some more tequila?'

'There is another bottle in the fridge.'

Cruise went to the kitchen to fetch the bottle. Axel started to talk about the apartment. He often does this. Was I happy with everything? Did I think anything was missing? For him, as a guest it was fine, but to live here. . . . There is nothing which needs to be done. I love the apartment and would change nothing. I tell him this, but he continues to make suggestion after suggestion, each more elaborate than the last.

They would not go dancing now. It was getting late and they had drunk and eaten much and were drugged by the atmosphere. When you are with friends, it is sometimes difficult to go out into the city and be with people you do not know. There is always a hostility which, at home with the curtains closed, you can ignore. But now I wish, in some ways, that they would go. I had planned, initially, for them to stay until dawn or later, as they often do. But when I thought that they would leave I changed my plans and the meal was eaten earlier than I would have liked. Now the evening did not have the balance I had intended. As time passed the meal had retreated into the periphery of the evening and the tequila and that discussion with Cruise, for me at least, had taken centre stage. At other times it is properly so – we all love food and it is right that it should be the focus of the evening on so many occasions. But often, too, it is something to get out of the way. If one of the others goes away for a while, when he returns we eat together solely in order to be able to consume more alcohol. As Cruise says: 'With food it goes better drinking.' If Axel goes to Denmark he always returns with a couple of bottles of Swedish punch and we spend the night drinking it with coffee. Or if Leppard makes a trip back to England, he will always bring back as much good quality single malt as he can carry – it is expensive here, for good stuff – and we eat small snacks throughout the evening but no meal. From the start this evening was theirs, I suppose. It was always to be.

There is a lull at some point in every evening. This is not a problem if everyone desires it. Cruise was reading. Axel was asleep. Leppard had gone running to the bathroom fifteen minutes before and was now taking a shower. I went back into the dining room and put on a collection of baroque tunes. They were, I felt, right for the moment. I opened one of the large windows and sat in the frame, on the ledge, sipping at a Margarita I had made myself, smoking a cigarette, staring down onto the street. A rat scuttled across the road. They are becoming a common sight in the city and when I put down some poison in my little wine cellar in the basement I found many dead bodies soon afterwards. They are big and only strong poison will kill them because they become immune to it. And when I put poison down I feel ill at ease, as if I have a skeleton in the cupboard, because you read of young children and family pets dying. I shudder when I think of the rats' capacity to transcend man's hostility to their species.

The street is quiet. The bars are open but there are few people out tonight. Strange because there are many new restaurants and nightclubs here in the fourth by the Naschmarkt and all summer they have been very busy. I suppose that the autumn is coming. I do not like winter in the city, though I remain here. It is very cold, it is unpleasant to leave the warmth of my apartment, to do anything at all. I spend too much time at home, alone with my thoughts. I should do something but beyond going to a coffee house, nothing appeals to me. Cruise likes to go to coffee houses with me. There is one, near the Hofburg, not a real coffee house like Museum or Hawelka, more a café, where you can sit in the window staring out onto the street. Leppard, surprisingly, likes to come there as well, though not Axel. The three of us sit there from lunchtime until it becomes dark, drinking tea with lemon, watching the people pass, saying little. And then we will meet Axel and go for some food and perhaps to a bar or to Hawelka where it is always busy at night and there are friends and we can forget the weather. Axel and Leppard like to ski and when they go – to St Anton or sometimes to Cortina – Cruise and I never see each other. Those times are very lonely here. I know I should go with them but I have not wished to ski since my parents died. There are too many memories.

Yes, the spring and the summer and early autumn are the best times to be in this town. Often we stay up all night, perhaps driving up to the Leopoldsberg for the dawn. From there you can see the entire city, spread out before you, and the Danube glowing in the half-light. I know people who have travelled the world but never seen the city from there, watched the sunrise from the Leopoldsberg. For them I feel sorry. They have not truly appreciated the beauty of our city.

As I was sitting there Cruise came to join me. He just sat in the other window, saying nothing. Then:

'I am sorry, my friend, for what I said to you earlier.'

'You have a point. Austria has yet to come to terms with its past. Or its present.'

'I went, yesterday, to the Karl-Marx-Hof.'

'I have only seen it from the bus.'

'I find it sad that socialism could create something so ugly.'

'Socialism also created the Hundertwasserhaus. Or allowed it to be built. It is a council house.'

'But occupied by lawyers and businessmen.'

'There is little justice, that is true.'

'They live in such poverty in the Karl-Marx-Hof. It is a tragedy that so many people should be neglected in the one place.'

'Do you think refurbishment would help?'

'That. But the building also represents the Austrian people's final courageous stand against Nazism. It should be honoured for that. When it was bombarded in '34 that was it for Austria. Hitler's entry was inevitable.'

'That does not say much for the Austrians, though. The Jews in the Warsaw ghetto fought to the end.'

'The Jews were condemned. The Austrians were given a choice.'

'A slight one.'

'A choice nevertheless. And to choose death over life may be wrong.'

I did not reply to this. He was right in saying that the Austrians' choice was mitigated by the circumstances to some extent. But how far I could not tell.

'What did your father do in the war? He would have been of the right age, no?'

'He was a soldier of some sort. I do not know what he did. He never spoke of it.'

'He never spoke of Hitler?'

Cruise talks like a psychiatrist sometimes. I think, after he was arrested in Italy, he was ill for a time. He told me once that he spent a year seeing various doctors. He knows that we are all traumatized by our history and whenever he discusses fascism with me uses this reflexive method he learnt then. Inviting me to talk my way deeper into my past. I have become adept at excusing myself.

'Shall I make some more coffee?'

Cruise nodded slowly and returned to his book.

The phone rang. Cruise answered it. This angered me slightly, although it was obviously for him. I do not mind him using the phone. But answering my phone with such casual assumption – as if I did not exist.

'My friend, some acquaintances of mine need to come here. Do you mind?'

'Of course not, Cruise.'

He muttered a few more words into the mouthpiece. I did not catch them, but they were not in German, anyway. He put the phone down and came back into the dining room and sat down again on the window ledge. Leppard appeared, fresh-faced and invigorated again after his shower.

'That's better. I needed that. Hey, my man, do you have anything else to drink? I've really had the tequila, you know.'

The evening, finally, had outpaced my plans. The initiative was theirs, now, and the best I could do was to go along with it. As I always have done. I simply pointed towards the kitchen. He knows the way.

'When will they come?'

I felt diminished now, as if I were an unwelcome guest in another's home, intruding upon their privacy but with no means of escape.

'Soon. They are nearby, but they must be careful in case they are being followed. For your sake and mine.'

'You know the way out.'

'Of course.'

The building backs onto an embassy compound and from my bedroom window it is easy to jump onto the low compound wall. If it is necessary they can hide and they will be safe.

'My friend.'

'Cruise.'

'They are dangerous people who are coming. They could cause you trouble with the police if they are followed.'

'Cruise, I am doing it for you so it does not matter.'

'Which is why I wish for you to know that they could bring trouble.'

'Forget it. They will come, they will stay, some time they will leave. It does not matter.'

Axel was awake. He came through and sat at the table, which I had cleared earlier, and lit a cigarette. We were smoking more than usual tonight and, although the open windows had cleared the air, the apartment smelt stale and unpleasant. He looked around the room with a kind of grim satisfaction. I followed his eyes but could not see why he was smiling.

Leppard spent a long time in the kitchen. When he returned it was with a tray on which was a collection of cold meats, cheeses, tomatoes, bread and pickles which he had taken from the fridge and the larder. He put it on the table and took some plates and cutlery from the sideboard and fetched two bottles of wine and a case of beer from the fridge. In some ways it is nice to be catered for in your own home and I suppose that it must reflect a certain depth of companionship that Leppard feels free to do this.

As we were sitting down Cruise's friends arrived. They were two Setovenes and dressed like Cruise in black polo necks and black trousers. They wore leather jackets which they did not take off. Cruise invited them to eat and drink but they refused and took only a whisky each and they sat drinking it in the sitting room. We four sat in the dining room at the table and began to eat. I remembered that I had in a cupboard some jars of herring. Leppard made a pained expression but Axel was pleased. He had, in fact, brought them himself from Denmark only a couple of weeks before.

'So who are your friends, Cruise?'

'They are from Carinthia. They are active on behalf of the minority there. They have been in Vienna for two weeks holding meetings with the Yugoslav guest workers here. They want to organize a strike by the guest workers in the winter.'

I nearly laughed out loud. There are nearly three hundred thousand guest workers in Austria, many of whom have no work and most of whom would never support a strike. On their pitiful wages it is all that they can do to earn enough for food from the work they get. And as one politician said recently, there are as many unemployed Austrians as there are guest workers: a simple answer to the so-called complex issue of unemployment. A stupid answer, of course, because the Austrians would never do that sort of work, but one which maintains the guest workers' fear of being deported.

'They will not strike, Cruise, no way.'

'But they might. And what if they did?'

'What?'

'Who would clear the snow? Who would sell the bourgeoisie of Vienna its newspapers? Who would do the really dirty work?'

'Probably other guest workers. The Turks, perhaps. They do not love the Yugoslavs.'

'But say they have their own reasons for striking. Who then? If the solidarity is there, who will do the work?'

'The army.'

'You know, you men have spent the entire evening arguing. How about it? Take a break. Let's have some love around here. Say, Axel, you primitive?'

'Sure, why not?'

Leppard rolled his eyes. Axel was concentrating fully on his fish. Even I did not know how he could eat it after being sick, but he seemed fine now.

'Leppard's right. Let's stop now.'

For a while we laughed and talked about things, drinking bottles of beer and eating the delicious cold meats and cheeses. Axel is a fair artist as well as an architect and one picture is of four of us in a bar, our muscles exaggerated and our clothes imagined so that we look like workers from a factory out at lunch. We enjoy such fantasies. We drink the beer straight from the bottle and slap the cheese and meat onto the bread in huge hunks, swaggering as we talk in parodies of the international figure of the proletarian hero. I would expect Cruise to object to this, but it is his own background we are celebrating. Leppard takes to it most easily. His parents became wealthy quite recently and until he was a teenager both were factory workers themselves. They set up their own business and immediately became successful. This is the reason Leppard came to Vienna, I am sure. He wished to escape the severe contradictions of class which exist in Britain. They are too painful for him. He finds himself unaccepted by workers and bourgeoisie alike and his own class, the new rich, are too neurotic, too self-obsessed to satisfy his curiosity, not to mention his taste. So he buries his own neuroses and there are few better ways to do this than beneath a language of which you are no master. Axel and, I imagine, myself are less convincing proles – though no less energetic and filled with bravado. The four of us love to strut through the city streets, shouting comments at old women or young girls: 'Hey, beautiful, come for a drink with us.' 'You, precious, we'll buy you an ice-cream if you bring some friends.'

And sometimes they do and we laugh and joke together before parting.

Leppard told the story, again, of how he and Axel and two Spanish girls spent a weekend in Prague soon after they first met here in Vienna. Both Cruise and I had heard the story many times, but this time it was told to introduce something which happened a week or two later when Leppard was in a café with one of the girls – Natalia – waiting for Axel. They had spent one month here, studying at a summer school. During this time they met many people and the high point was the visit to Czechoslovakia. There they had an adventure with a Russian named Igor who held a West German passport and said he was on holiday with a friend. He drove a Mercedes 190 and seemed to have a great deal of money. This was before *Glasnost* and they had been slightly suspicious of him from the start, when he spoke with the waiter and they were not allowed to pay for their meal. He drove them around the city and took them to places which they would otherwise not have found. Even to the Russian Embassy in the hills above the town. Early in the morning they were stopped by the police, but Igor, who was drunk, spoke only a few words to the policemen in Russian and they were given a police escort back to their hotel.

With the 'KGB' man as their starting point, Leppard and Natalia constructed a conspiracy at the centre of which they alone were the unwitting innocents. As the conversation progressed they drew all the individuals they had met into the plot and assigned them roles. An American friend was with the CIA, the Italians on the course were Mafia people, the Spaniards were Fascists, agents of Franco's supporters seeking to reintroduce a dictatorship with help from Austrian neo-Nazis – of whom I, apparently, was one. Axel arrived and the construct collapsed. His solid, Danish common sense found the affair foolish and he could not participate. Even now he found the telling of the story embarrassing.

The tale loses something in the telling, I imagine, but the point remains:

'It takes only the smallest iota of imagination to create a fiction substantial enough to draw the world into itself. We all have our fantasies. Axel's is that the world is a well-ordered place which simply needs a little decorating and some good design to brighten it up. Yours, Cruise, is that the owners of property exploit everyone else and that such exploitation can be changed.'

'That's no fantasy, Leppard.'

'It's a fiction and you bring in evidence to support it.'

'And what's your fiction, your fantasy?'

'Aha! That's for others to judge.'

'And what is mine?'

There was an instant of discomfort as I said this.

'You, my man? Your fantasy is the most delightful of all. You firmly believe that if we all eat and drink enough, the whole world will go away and we'll all be fine.'

I was not sure how to take this.

'I mean that in the most positive possible way.'

I grinned at him, but he could see that I was still rather puzzled.

Next door, in the sitting room, the two Carinthians were still sitting in silence, occasionally sipping at their drinks. I could see them through the door from where I was, at the table. I was surprised that Cruise had said so little to them. He appeared angry with them in some way. Or more probably he was torn between his cultural – or political – loyalty to them and the loyalties associated with his friendships. Though more than merely peripheral to these three, I have never truly been a part of their brotherhood. It is impenetrable to outsiders, stronger than blood. Like the best friendships, it has survived much strain in its time. There have, I know, been bitter confrontations – the worst one between Axel and Leppard over a girl. These are caused by the very frivolity they enjoy. There are times when Axel will feel that Leppard is taking him and Cruise too much for granted. Or Leppard, in turn, will be angry that the others are not taking him seriously enough. Or Cruise, mindful of his Ph.D., his mother's expectations of him, his advancing age, will sternly admonish the other two – and himself – on the need for seriousness and spiritual growth. Look at our friend J—, he has developed in this last year; we must work harder or we will be left behind. You, Leppard, must stop this foolishness and find a regular girl. You, Axel, must learn to hold your drink or not drink at all. And you, Cruise, are full of shit, comes the inevitable response before they go out and get drunk again and wind up the professionals who work outside the block where Cruise lives, on the Gürtel, the highway which orbits the inner city and which has brothels all round it. Frequently their company makes me feel very lonely indeed.

Leppard and I had just thrown down our knives and were lighting cigarettes when Cruise stood and ran to the toilet. A few moments later we heard him being sick and Leppard laughed loudly again.

'Three down. Just one to go, my man.'

'Not me, friend. I can hold my booze. You children need some practice.'

We made some jokes about Cruise's sudden exit. Probably it was not the drink, but the sight of Axel with his raw fish which made Cruise ill. No, it was listening to Leppard's stupidity. That would churn the strongest stomach. Or was I sure I had prepared the food properly before and washed my hands after that 'nap' I took earlier?

Cruise returned, a frown on his forehead.

'Never, never before has this happened to me. I think I must be getting old.'

'Admit it, Cruise. You got caught out. You just can't handle the pace these days, that's all.'

'Perhaps, friend, perhaps.'

Next door the Slovenes were staring at us, not understanding the excitement. I found them disturbing. Their silence was almost threatening. The others seemed to feel their intrusion as well. All three looked uncomfortable now, and restless. Axel had gone to the window and was standing, looking outside. Leppard was examining his fingernails. And Cruise, bright and alert, was looking around him, nodding, almost waiting for something to happen. Tentatively, I cleared my throat.

'Why do we not go somewhere? For a walk and maybe to a bar?'

Cruise, Leppard and Axel looked at me. Then at each other. Cruise's face was the first to light up and the rest of us grinned too.

I got up and switched off a few lights and put on the dishwasher.

Then I got a jacket to wear because it was a little cold outside. Cruise spoke to the Carinthians and then to me.

'They would prefer to remain here where they will be safe. Do you mind if they stay? I've told them that they must not move from where they are sitting. Not even to piss.'

I was concerned. There are things of value here and it did not seem to me that Cruise knew these friends well. But I could hardly insist that they leave. I had welcomed them into my house as guests and to send them away would be wrong.

'They know the way out?'

'Yes, I've told them.'

Outside it was even colder than I had expected. Some of the bars were starting to shut. If we wanted to drink there were other places, however, which were open later or all night. The restaurant where Cruise works is near here and does not even open until after midnight. For now we were happy just to walk and talk, pleased to have a change of atmosphere and scenery. If we had not had so much to drink I might have suggested that we drive up to the Leopoldsberg. It was a clear night and the sunrise would be worth seeing. We walked through the Naschmarkt and past the Secession building towards Karlsplatz. From the underground entrance we cut across to Karlskirche and sat in front of the church for a while. Then we went through the Kärntnerstrasse to the centre of the city. There were still people walking around the streets and in St Stephen's Square, the Gothic heart of the city. From there we walked eastwards until we found ourselves in Reimergasse where there is a café-bar I go to sometimes. It is a good place where they play opera the whole time and loudly. Many opera stars go there after performing and the atmosphere is friendly and artistic. But the doors were closing when we arrived so we walked on to the Ringstrasse and south, past the hotel where Hitler stayed in '38, and then back towards the fourth.

'OK, let's go to the restaurant.'

'You sure? You'll have to play.'

Cruise plays the piano well and in the restaurant where he works there is always live music from Yugoslavia. A plaque on the wall says that Wagner used to have a regular table there.

When we arrived, Cruise was greeted noisily and warmly and as he was taken to the piano to play we were given a good table and beers and offered food which we declined. Cruise taught himself to play the piano and cannot read music. He is very good and plays Balkan folk tunes by ear. We three sat there, listening to his playing and clapping the beat in time with the other customers when we could, but getting lost mostly, and laughing about their music.

Eventually he was allowed to stop playing and a wicker basket was passed around for contributions. The owner of the place came and sat with us, telling us that Cruise was his best waiter and a good friend to have.

An Austrian acquaintance of mine turned up just as we were thinking of going. He insisted that we stay for another drink and ordered two bottles of champagne. I did not want to stay because I knew that Axel would have no interest in him, Cruise would soon come to despise him and Leppard would argue with him. His name is Otto and he is a student. He comes from a very rich, aristocratic Vienna family. He is friends with the Habsburgs and many other European monarchs and he mentions their names incessantly. That did not even matter so much, but I told him once about my friends and Cruise and Leppard he particularly wanted to meet. He imagines himself a writer and paid for a collection of his stories and poems to be printed by a vanity publisher. He carries copies of it with him everywhere to give to people he meets and hardly knows. Cruise insisted that we stay a little longer. He always likes to meet new friends.

'It seems that we have something in common, colleagues.'

'And what's that, my man?'

'Well, I understand from our friend, here, that you, Leppard are a novelist and that you, Cruise, are a poet. Whereas I myself am both.'

This was what I had feared. Neither Leppard nor Cruise ever refer to themselves as either novelists or poets, not even in jest. Leppard's response was predictable.

'Really, and do you do both at the same time or do you prefer to alternate?'

'Well, I have two novels on the boil at the moment and I do try to pull together at least one poem every day, though I forgive myself as long as I scribble down some notes, at least.'

Seeing Leppard's face, and being rather more generous, Cruise broke in:

'And have you had anything published?'

'As a matter of fact I have a copy of my collection with me.'

He rooted in his jacket pocket for the paperback and handed it to Cruise who started to leaf through it. Leppard rested his chin on Cruise's shoulder and stared at the book with open contempt.

'Of course, as with all literature, it needs careful reading. Take it, take it home with you, Cruise. And Leppard, I shall send you a copy. Perhaps you would like to review it.'

'Yeah, sure, why not.'

A glint in his eye. I could just imagine what he would say in his most cutting manner. I did not care. I do not like Otto, or his friends. They still think of Vienna as their private property and treat it and its inhabitants as such. Had I not told him that Cruise was his nation's most famous poet in exile – a lie – he would not have spoken to him even now.

'So what do you write about, Leppard?'

'Love and politics.'

'Not love and death? No, rather clichéd in our time, are they not. Have you had anything published? No? Well, not to worry, everyone's chance comes to them. You simply must keep plugging away. But you, you are well known, are you not, Cruise. I don't believe there is a translation of your works in German yet – perhaps I could arrange it. My cousin is the director of P– Verlag, he is always keen to look at fresh talent, either from home or abroad. So, where do you drink, as a rule? I do prefer the seedier side of the city. There is so much more material for the close observer, don't you think . . .'

I soon stopped listening and talked with Axel about his new project. He is to design an apartment for an American who wants a home from home, but with an Austrian feel to it. By this, we decide that he does not mean something in the Jugendstil tradition. More probably the American is thinking in terms of Mozart. Prints of that Venetian artist would be in order, and furniture of the period – though made new by Axel. Of course, the American would want all mod cons. Axel is partners with two Swedes and a Norwegian who specialize in the provision of 'Integrated Audio-Visual Centres' for the rich. These are huge and complex affairs by which an apartment becomes a temple to the modern age. Televisions, video recorders, sound systems are connected up and operated by remote control. Lights which switch themselves on and off depending upon who is in the room and whether it is day or night. Computer controlled airconditioning, telephones which are linked to the lighting and which, when they ring, turn down the volume of the television or music. Axel's responsibility is to make those masses of wire and circuitry attractive and neat. Of course, he does it well. Such is his pragmatism. The American has given him a huge budget and the flat is very large. He will use it for entertaining business customers – flying them to Vienna for two or three days to see an opera and the Spanish Riding School – so everything must be lavish. The apartment will have everything possible to make brief stays comfortable. As we talk, Axel's fantasy grows larger and larger. Jacuzzis, a solarium, a computer with which the American can send messages home or check share prices, a fax and everything else a good office has. He would write to a friend in San Francisco, asking for catalogues of all the things one finds in an American home. We are so backward here.

Eventually, realizing that he was the butt of Cruise and Leppard's sarcasm, Otto stood to leave. He nodded rather stiffly to me and when he had gone we laughed long and hard. But he had upset Cruise who just kept saying over and over:

'What an asshole. What a total asshole.'

Soon we wanted to leave too so Cruise paid the bill with the money he had earned from playing the piano and we went. As we walked slowly back to my apartment we noticed that there was a dim glow around the edges of the buildings on the Wienzeile. It was nearly dawn and we had done it again, stayed up all night as so many times before.

Even before we went into the building I sensed that something was wrong. Perhaps the fact that some lights were on which I had turned out before we left. I do not know. When I tried to open the door it was jammed. The door had been bolted from the inside. I rang the bell and then Cruise started to knock softly and called to the Slovenes in a hoarse whisper. I turned and ran back down the stairs. I would be able to get into the cellars by the service entrance and from my little wine cellar up the back stairs to the kitchen of my apartment. Cruise and Leppard followed me but Axel stayed behind, ringing the bell insistently. I unlocked the cellar door and went through to the other door which was open. At the top of the stairs there was a light coming from the kitchen. I had switched it off. I slowly went up the stairs. In the kitchen there were tins and boxes on the floor and some jars and bottles had been smashed. Cruise was behind me, furious.

'I swear to you they will die for this. I will kill them with my own two hands.'

In the dining room two chairs were broken and the contents of the sideboard and cabinets strewn over the whole room. The sitting room had been searched, though not as violently as the dining room. The coffee table was broken, one leg snapped off. My painting was undamaged but was askew on the wall. I opened the door to the corridor which leads to the bedrooms and to my father's study, at the end. From the doorway I could see that the study door had been kicked down. It is always kept locked. Cruise pushed past me and I shouted to him.

'No!'

But it was too late. He stood in the doorway of the study, staring at its contents. I walked slowly towards him and Leppard came quickly past me and past Cruise, into the small room. Axel had joined us and remained behind me as I leaned against the door-frame, looking in at the desk and the possessions which my father had left there, preserved for nearly half a century. I could not look at Cruise whose eyes I could feel fixed on me now, searching for my reaction. Leppard was fingering the material of my father's uniform which was folded neatly, as always, on top of the chest of drawers.

'Why, why did you not tell us of this?'

'How could I? How could I tell you?'

'Your father's?'

I nodded. I felt the blood draining from my head and the tears pricking at my eyes.

'Why have you kept all of this here?'

'He was my father. What could I do?'

'Yes. He was your father.'

'What should I have done. He was my father. I loved him, as anyone loves a father. He was my father.'

'He was a Nazi. He was an SS officer. A Colonel.'

'Do you think I have not had to live with that? Do you think I approve of that?'

'Where did he serve? This is the Death's Head emblem. Was he a prison camp guard? Where? Mauthausen?'

My voice cracked as I answered.

'Belsen.'

'Shit. But why have you kept it? Why?'

'Can you not see? I told you before. My grandfather was a court servant. My father was his son. He was brought up to serve. And after . . . until . . . that is all he did. He just followed orders, there was no choice anyway, you said so, Cruise. You said that.'

'No choice. And where did his wealth – your wealth – come from?'

'I do not *know*.'

'Did you never ask yourself: How could my father, a simple man, be so wealthy?'

'Even I did not see the inside of this room until his death. I never knew of this. He could never have risked that. It was dangerous enough for him to carry on living in Vienna. He should have gone to America or Australia. The strain of the secret killed him in the end.'

'Poor man. And how many did he rob and kill? Hundreds? Thousands? You are a fool. You should have destroyed all of this. Or told us when you found it. I remember, now, how little you said when he died. You should have told me.'

'He was wrong, but he was my father.'

'Yes, until his death. Enjoy your aesthetic pleasures, friend. They are not for me.'

Cruise spat on the floor of the study and pushed past me roughly. Leppard followed him out without even looking at me. I turned to Axel, appealing to him to understand. But he shook his head, his disgust evident. And they were gone and I was left with the silence of my father's apartment.

After they had gone I cried for nearly an hour, sitting in my father's seat, leaning my head on his desk. The contempt in Cruise's glare, the disgust written on Axel's face, these things burn my mind even now.

This room has haunted me. In a letter, left with his lawyer, my father told me what to expect. At first I wanted to destroy it all. I hated him as I had learnt to hate the Nazis for what they had done to my country. But as the months and then years passed and I came here daily to sit and think, to sit here at my father's desk, surrounded by his mementoes, his uniform and weapons, his papers, his medals, the excuses started to come to me. There must be many Austrians whose fathers were death camp guards. Not all of them as courageous as my father in his decision to stay. There were many alive still who had killed Jews and taken their possessions. I was not alone. And what should I have done? My father's money – and there was enough – was legally saved in Austrian banks. I had no evidence to suggest that it had once been gold in a Swiss vault. None at all. And the photographs of my father, being awarded the Iron Cross by Hitler, meeting with Himmler and others, these made me feel proud of his achievements, my simple father. Until the war, after the end of the Empire, my father had been no one. A servant without masters. The war gave him a purpose. And if he had refused to serve, what then? A prison camp? Death? He only wanted to get on in life, just wanted a life without trouble like any other Austrian. And all of these objects were immaculately preserved. He had cared for them. In those long hours in this study, polishing and brushing, reading through his commendations and personal telegraph messages from the Führer. His Führer. This had been his life after the war.

Now, for the first time, I try on his uniform. It is a little tight and my hair is much longer than my father's in the photographs. But in the mirror I can see a resemblance. I am his son and I carry his clothes with a grace he would have recognized. And now I am sitting again at his desk, reading his documents and diaries over and over, wondering how it must have been for him after the war was lost, when the Jews were crying for blood and the Germans were betraying their own people. My friends, Cruise, Axel, Leppard, they could never understand this. They have no reason to fear their pasts. They have nothing to shame them in the eyes of others. They would not understand my feelings now. Proud of my father. Truly proud, without guilt, for the first time. Proud, even, though timidly, of myself for being his son. The son he would have wanted to have if it had all been different.

Leppard wrote, in his novel: 'When you read a book, it is your own voice that your mind hears. If that voice is in harmony with your mind's own expectations then its dictates will vindicate your most secret fantasies.' When I eat food cooked by another, I think always in terms of what I would have done, how I would have done it. My father's thoughts, as written in his diary on the day the German armies surrendered, they come to me now. His pistol, loaded, I know, with a single bullet, has rested there always, there on the edge of the desk. A constant reminder to him of the options which exist. 'If, as they say, the Führer is dead, I must nevertheless fulfil my duty to the German People, to myself. I will go on. My courage will be unwavering.' And in those words, my deepest, most carefully concealed desires find their affirmation.

I will keep the apartment as it is, as Axel has designed it. The Hundertwasser as well. Perhaps, as Cruise says, he is partly Jewish. But above all else, he is Austrian. And that is what matters.

*Breakfast
was simple*

Breakfast was simple but distinctive: black olives with mint and lemon juice sprinkled over them; feta cheese, tomatoes and Turkish bread; hard-boiled eggs; mineral water to drink.

'Turkish breakfast,' said Medar, as he speared an olive and ate it, carefully spitting the stone back onto the fork and delivering it to the side of his plate, fastidious as ever. Reid nodded slowly. It was all he could do to sit upright and sip occasionally at his water. Conversation was beyond him. They had been to a party the night before. In the third. Then they had gone to a couple of bars before returning to Medar's apartment near the Ottakringerstrasse, in the sixteenth. There they had drunk a litre of Austrian rum between them before falling asleep as dawn approached. Medar is from East Anatolia and he prides himself on his ability to drink a great deal and then to get up early the following morning as if nothing out of the ordinary has occurred. On this occasion they had slept for only three hours and Reid was not sober enough to feel hungover, not drunk enough to enjoy the feeling.

After a while spent watching Medar eat, Reid went through to the kitchen, opened the fridge and returned with a jar of hot pickled peppers which he handed to the Turk.

'Colleague, your arse will never forgive you.'

'My stomach's going to be happy in the meantime, though, friend.'

Medar shrugged, untwisted the lid, took out a pepper and handed the jar back to Reid. Reid held it in his hand for a moment, reading the label, before putting it down and breaking a piece of bread from the loaf which he dipped into the jar before eating.

'I remember when I first tasted these bastards. I ate half a jar one night and spent most of the next day on the toilet. I didn't spot the connection so I did the same again two days later. Then I realized.'

'And now, colleague, you are a hard-assed man, no?'

'Hard-assed enough, friend.'

He put a pepper in his mouth, chewed it thoroughly and swallowed, nodded and smiled.

Medar's apartment is furnished according to a minimalist taste which reflects his approach to life. In one corner of the main room there is his desk, at which he and Reid were eating. In the opposite corner there is the spare mattress upon which Reid had slept and in front of the windows stands a large wooden cabinet upon which there is an expensive stereo. Apart from that the room is empty. Medar's music collection is appropriate to the decor: lots of Miles Davis, Herbie Hancock, Archie Shepp and Don Cherry and, for when Medar is alone, a collection of bootlegs of a Kurdish jazz band whose name Reid could not pronounce and which he found too strange to his ears, even by the standards of Medar's normal tastes. Reid disliked silence so he decided to put on some music. After a few minutes of flicking through the albums and cassettes he finally found what he was looking for, what he always played if he awoke in his own apartment in the seventh. 'A poem which was written by myself and which is dedicated to my grandmother and the revolutionary struggle which transpired during the sixties . . .' The introduction to *Mama Rose* was guaranteed to bring a smile to Medar's face. They cleared the plates and the uneaten food from the desk and, as Reid started washing the dishes, Medar said that he was going to shave.

The kitchen of Medar's apartment doubles as a bathroom – there is an extra sink and a shower in the corner – and while Reid washed the dishes he watched Medar as he studied his reflection and then applied shaving soap from a tube in thick stripes across his skin. Reid could hear the rasp of the razor blade. Medar noticed that he was being observed and said: 'Where I am from we take shaving seriously, colleague. Shaving is important.'

'Unless you have a beard, my man.'

'Only intellectuals have beards.'

Reid punched him quite hard in the ribs and they laughed because Reid had been growing a beard for five weeks and Medar was always making jokes about it, saying that in comparison to the Turkish, the English were like little girls when it came to hair. Then Reid put on a different record and smoked a cigarette while Medar finished getting ready to go out.

Usually on Saturdays the two of them ran a stall at the flea market. They would sell sunglasses and T-shirts or anything they liked. They made no money from it now, nor did they need to. It was how they had earned a living when they first came to Vienna and setting up the stall every Saturday was a habit which they chose to hold on to, a reminder of what it had been like trying to survive in the city without permits, when the only way is to work illegally. As well as this, though, running the stall was a good way to spend the day and they met many people by doing so. Most of their friends had been made that way. On this morning, however, neither of them was in the mood to take his goods to the market. When the necessity exists no longer, humility becomes either a luxury or a chore and as the weather was hot and sunny they decided to take the day off. They would, however, go to the market, or at least to the area, to meet some of their friends. At half-past nine they left Medar's apartment and took the tram to the Rathaus underground station and from there the U2 to Karlsplatz. Like many other people in Vienna, Reid and Medar seldom bought tickets for travel. Drivers do not check the passengers and there are few conductors. There are inspectors, however, and if someone is caught, they must pay a small fine. Medar and Reid belonged to a group of people, each of whom paid a small sum into a contingency fund every month. If a member of the group was caught travelling without a ticket their fine would be paid out of the fund. As long as the group members were reasonably careful, the result was cheaper travel for them all. Reid could, of course, have afforded to buy a season ticket at the full price, but such games with the authorities pleased him.

At Karlsplatz they left the underground and walked a short way along the Wienzeile to a café by the Naschmarkt where they always met a friend of theirs for a coffee and perhaps some food at about ten. Christa was already there when they arrived, sitting with an Irishman who she introduced as Feargal. Feargal was originally from Cork, he said, but he had lived in London for some time and had been touring around Europe for the previous two years. He had just spent six months in Frankfurt but he did not like the city much, although he had found a good job there, working as a barman in an expensive nightclub. Christa had discovered him asleep on a bench in the Kärtnerstrasse late the night before. Typically for her – for all three of them – she had woken him up and invited him to stay at the apartment she shares with her brother. They enjoyed such gestures and, indeed, Reid had an Australian guest at the time who had been staying with him for two months already.

When the coffees came for Reid and Medar, Feargal mentioned what a problem he was having finding a place to stay. Medar replied: 'No one said to you, colleague, that life would be easy.'

Feargal's mouth opened wide with anger and he did not answer. Reid said: 'Medar's only joking, friend. If there's a man who believes in taking life easy, he's the one.'

Reid knew that Medar, with his un-European attitudes, took some getting used to and he wanted to defuse the situation before any hostility took root. In truth Medar had meant the words in all seriousness. Despite his generosity and warm nature, Medar has a didactic approach to everyone he meets and if he sees the opportunity to speak some words of wisdom, painful or not, he employs it. When Reid said this Feargal smiled, but he was quiet for some time.

Christa, who was a student of fashion design at the School of Applied Arts, had been in trouble with her tutor. Earlier in the week it had been the anniversary of the Annexation of Austria by Hitler in March 1938. One of Reid, Medar and Christa's friends was an old Jew called Franz Lasker. Reid had bought Franz's apartment from him two years before and the old man now lived in a nursing home. Christa had told her tutor about Franz in the past and he wanted her to bring him to the school to deliver a guest lecture. Franz always refused to be stereotyped by his Austrian compatriots and Christa was uncertain whether inviting him to speak was a good idea. The invitation did, however, present Franz with a rare opportunity to spend the day away from the nursing home and the strict medical regime there. He was never allowed either coffee or tobacco because, the doctors said, it was bad for his circulation. This was something against which Franz, with the support of Reid, Christa and Medar, had rebelled strongly. As Medar was fond of saying, Franz should have been squeezing his life dry, not allowing it to evaporate away. The doctors were firm but as soon as Christa picked him up from the home, Franz demanded that they go for a cup of coffee before doing anything else. It was his first in over a year and his enjoyment was so apparent that Christa bought him another and then a third. By then the old man was shaking like a leaf and she decided against taking him to the school. She rang her tutor and told him that Mr Lasker had died in his sleep the night before. She was too upset by this tragedy to come into school. Then they went to a tobacconist where she bought Franz a pipe and his favourite tobacco and they spent the rest of the day driving around Vienna, from one coffee house to the next. It was the first time he had seen most of the places they visited in twenty-five years or more and both of them thoroughly enjoyed the outing. The problem was that Franz's nurse, worried that he had not returned by noon, called Christa's tutor to find out what had happened. Christa's tutor was angry with his student.

'But what annoyed him most was when I told him what I thought of him anyway, wheeling out old Jews just to soothe his conscience. He's an old Nazi, you know. A real one. He couldn't do much about it, though, because the principal's a friend of my dad's. Actually, I did tell Franz that I might go and see him today. What do you guys think?'

While Christa related her story Reid observed Feargal closely. He was young with smooth features, short-cropped hair and stubble. He had a large ear-ring in each ear and his eyes were a deep brown – almost black – and intense. He wore black boots, black trousers and a black polo neck sweater such as Medar always wears, and looked for all the world, thought Reid, like a refugee from the set of a sixties TV series. The most striking thing about him, and what convinced Reid that Feargal was no mere fashion victim come home, was the plain steel hook which was attached in place of a hand to his forearm. Feargal noticed Reid's stare and, after tapping the hook twice on the table, he smiled, raised his arm and scratched his nose with the hook in a theatrical gesture and said: 'Legacy of a misspent youth, I'm afraid.'

Medar broke in and said: 'Be proud of your misspent youth, colleague. A truly misspent youth would be one which left no legacy for others to see. I too have my own legacy.'

He lifted his sweater to show Feargal the lumpy, hairless mass of scar tissue on the right side of his lower abdomen, where he had been shot whilst playing with friends during his military service in Turkey.

'Not quite the same, though, is it?'

'Not as dramatic, colleague, but evidence enough. Scars are honourable. Be proud.'

'So, what are you doing in Vienna, friend?'

Feargal seemed surprised that Reid should ask him this.

'I'm just passing through, you know. Seeing what there is to see, see if maybe I feel like staying a while.'

'Reid's a writer, Feargal, tell him what you really want to do.'

Reid shot a glance of annoyance at Christa. When he first arrived in Vienna he had fostered dreams of becoming a novelist, but those aspirations had soon been suffocated by the need to earn money, by his desire to spend time with friends, by the fact that his work as a journalist at the English-language radio station placed such demands on his creativity that there was little left for a work of fiction. Reid noticed that Feargal did not seem any happier about Christa's comment than he was and said: 'Christa's exaggerating when she calls me a writer, friend.'

'I've only toyed with the notion myself. I'd not want to be a writer so much as a poet. But it's just an idea, you know. I never will be, I expect.'

'No harm in trying, friend. There was a time when perhaps I'd have liked to write. I don't know.'

'You know nothing, colleague.'

'As Medar so rightly says: I know nothing.'

'You know nothing because you deserve to know nothing.'

'Whereas Medar, on the other hand, has a monopoly on the truth.'

'The truth may not be owned. It comes to those who know best how to employ it.'

'So you're telling me that the truth, although it can't be owned, can be employed?'

'Your attempts at rhetoric are laughable, colleague. You should stick to journalism and leave philosophy to the philosophers of this world.'

'I know nothing.'

Reid pushed away his empty cup and reached for Christa's packet of cheap Austrian cigarettes, leaned back in his chair and lit the cigarette with Medar's Zippo.

'You see: always our colleague tries other people's cigarettes, food, drinks. He is concerned that his own choice has excluded him from some esoteric pleasure essential to his future contentment and well-being. Reid: you pride yourself on the breadth of your experience of life, but the tragic reality is that your experience lacks depth and texture. You know nothing because you merely play at learning. You learn nothing and you play-act your life.'

'Jesus Christ, what did I do to deserve this?'

Feargal looked happy for the first time since Medar and Reid had arrived.

'No one said to you, colleague, that life would be easy.'

Medar laughed and slapped the Irishman on the back. 'Good, good, colleague. You, perhaps, could be a writer.'

Medar's didacticism focuses particularly on his friends' and acquaintances' abilities to fulfil their respective ambitions. He is at an advantage in this because his own ambitions are very simple: he wishes to marry, have three children – sons – and buy a motor-bike. When the children are grown up he will travel back to Turkey with his wife and his motorbike and live on money sent to him by his sons. Neither Reid nor Christa had any clear desires for the future but the fact that those desires went beyond simply wishing to marry and settle down meant that Medar was free to say as he wished regarding their abilities, Reid's in particular. He said to Feargal: 'What you should understand, however, is that it is not possible to become a writer or a poet, as our colleague imagines. Either you are already a writer or you are not. What Reid calls becoming a writer is, in truth, the process of discovering that you are one already.'

Reid, believing that any ambition may be fulfilled given the time, money and commitment, said: 'Don't listen to this asshole, friend.

You got something to say: say it. You don't: get pissed instead and it'll come to you soon enough. Anyone can write if that's what they want. You just got to make the choice.'

'The existentialist speaks, colleague, what do you make of that if you are not overwhelmed by the profundity of his statements?'

Feargal only shrugged.

'Anyway, Medar, you haven't told me what you've been up to yourself. I haven't seen you for a week.'

Medar carefully tapped a cigarette out of Reid's packet, lit it and inhaled deeply, waited for a moment and exhaled before answering Christa. Reid looked at him sardonically. He was used to Medar's behaviour when he is aware that he is at the centre of everyone's attention. When he has a story to relate he likes to make the most of it.

'This has been an interesting week for me. Thursday night in particular was interesting, most interesting. I arranged to meet some colleagues in a bar near my apartment. It is a shit bar where many pimps go, but it was convenient for us. We had some drinks and a good conversation, but the friends had to leave relatively early. I did not feel like going home and it was too late to go somewhere else, so I stayed and ordered another beer. Beside me at the next table there was a very attractive Hungarian girl who was also quite friendly. I spoke to her while I was waiting for my drink and we seemed to be getting on quite well, but the barmaid, when she returned with my drink, said to me: "Leave this poor girl alone, Turk, she doesn't want to talk to you." I was insulted, as you can imagine, so as she walked away from the table, I said to her in quite a loud voice: "You are so ugly, tart, no one would fuck even your arse." This she did not like, especially, I think, because many of the other guests laughed when they heard me. She threw a heavy glass ashtray at me, but it missed and smashed against the wall. I got up, hit her and knocked her out. KO with just one punch. She should have known better: where I am from it does not matter to us if it is a man or a woman who comes to us and wants to fight. We always accept the challenge. Anyway, two of the pimps came to me and said I should go outside with them. The Hungarian girl followed us out and the pimps said: "OK, if you leave now we will forget about this." I was happy to go, because there were two of them and also because it was a very good night to go for a romantic walk under the stars with this girl.'

Reid and Christa laughed and Feargal smiled lopsidedly.

Christa asked: 'So, is this the new love?'

'Unfortunately not. She does not like Vienna because, she says, it is too violent. She will return to Hungary next week. I have, anyway, my regular whore who I see once a week if I have the money. Her pimp does not like me because I tire her out too much, but he is scared, I think, that she will leave him for me if he tries to stop me seeing her. I pay my money in any case and he is not tough enough to worry me.'

'Medar has a strange idea of the romantic, that's for sure.'

'Nothing is certain, colleague. Certainties died with God. There is only fluidity and flux.'

'You sure?'

'Yes, colleague, I am positive.'

With the weather being so good they did not want to stay in the café for too long and Reid did not feel like going to the flea market and fighting his way through the crowds. Knowing that it would take them a long time to decide what to do instead, he ordered himself a beer, partly to stave off the hangover he could feel coming on and partly as a matter of habit: Reid liked to drink alcohol on Saturday mornings to remind himself that the weekend was underway and on Sunday afternoons to remind himself that it was nearly over. The others ordered drinks as well, even Medar which, Reid thought, was unusual for him. Normally Medar would say that one should wait until sunset before starting to drink alcohol and on Saturday mornings he would sit with a glass of tea and a superior smile watching Reid and Christa as they drank their beers, uncomfortable beneath his disapproving gaze. It remains an academic point with him: if Reid were to drink from the moment he awoke, Medar would still consume more alcohol between sunset and midnight than Reid ever could in an entire day. Medar asked Reid: 'Colleague, do you by some miracle have any food at your apartment?'

'You know me, Medar.'

'So, then. We should go to the Naschmarkt, buy some food for tonight which we can leave at your apartment, and then, slowly, we can go somewhere.'

'OK, my man, fine by me. But where?'

'Feargal, do you know how long you're going to stay in Vienna?'

'I can't say, Christa. If I was going to stay a while I'd need to find some work, not straightaway, but soon. Medar just mentioned, though, that you need a permit to work here, so perhaps I'll go back to Germany or to Italy instead.'

'That's true, friend, but the issue of work permits in Austria is an academic one, whatever the authorities think: you need a permit to get work, but you need work to get a permit. There should be no problem.'

'You can stay at my place for as long as you want anyway, Feargal. Money's not a problem either, not while you're here.'

'Thank you, Christa, but I'd not want to put you out at all. If I do stay I'll sort something out, and a place to stay.'

Medar raised his right hand to his chest, fingers out straight, and pushed the air away sharply in a swooping, characteristic gesture of dismissal.

'Colleague, whilst you are here, you are our friend. You must accept our hospitality or you will offend us.'

'We'll see.'

'The point being that we should do something today which will show Feargal something of our city.'

'Christa is so thoughtful. Listen to her, colleague, here I am: a Turk. Here is Reid: from London. And Vienna is our city. Not all Austrians are so courteous.'

'Is there a problem here with that?'

'Occasionally. Only yesterday Reid and I were in a shop in the ninth district and the assistant addressed me with the familiar form instead of the polite form one should use with strangers, especially with customers.'

'But Medar was good. He asked her if he knew her from somewhere. Had they perhaps eaten dinner together earlier in the week, or was it her who'd cooked him breakfast that morning? She was so stupid she still didn't get it, though, and I had to explain it to her and make her apologize. It was funny.'

'People should show some respect. I have an MA from the University of Vienna, I am a professional, no?'

'In so far as you can make a career out of doing nothing, I suppose so.'

'This colleague has a fine sense of irony. He sits at a desk all day copying news articles from foreign papers and pretending that they are his own work.'

'My work requires a great deal of skill, Medar.'

'To plagiarize so well that the copy is indistinguishable from the original requires a special talent, that much is true, but a talent for what?'

Reid took Medar by both shoulders and gave him a wet kiss on the cheek, a clear sign that enough was enough, and the four of them lapsed into silence.

Reid only went sightseeing when friends visited him from London and even then his tours were made in such a desultory way that on the second day he would give up. For him the best way to learn about a city was to meet the people who lived there, to have dinner with them, get drunk, go to a coffee house. Buildings could always be pointed out on the way. The only thing Reid did like to do was visit the occasional gallery, but in Vienna in March many of the exhibitions are shut or only partly open while they are prepared for the summer season. All sightseeing was a futile activity for Reid and he suspected the Irishman would see things that way. The first to speak was Feargal.

'Would there be a zoo in Vienna?'

'Not if you have a conscience.'

'Or maybe only if you have a bad conscience.'

'It's not a very good zoo.'

'I like zoos however they are. Not in themselves, so much, but for what they tell you about the city and the people who live there. There's a park in Bolzano, where I was just last week, and they have an old bear there, kept in a pit of some sort. The poor creature's mad with the size of it and the heat, you know. Truly it's a sad sight. But the thing is parents still take their kids along to see it. Well, you only need a history book to tell you that the Italians are as barbaric as they come, that way, but still . . .'

'I hate to think what Vienna's zoo will tell you about the Viennese, friend. What do you say, Medar?'

'Zoos, I do not like zoos. All these peculiar creatures locked up. I do not like this. However, Feargal is our guest . . .'

'The zoo, then.'

They finished their drinks and Reid paid the bill. Then they went over the road to the market where they would buy food for the evening.

Whilst he did not enjoy cooking, Reid loved to go shopping in the Naschmarkt with Medar. Many of the stallholders are Turkish and Medar knows most of them by name. He walks from one stall to the next greeting the owners and telling them what he thinks of the produce they have on display: 'These would not be fit for the goats, colleague.' 'The price of these tomatoes is reasonable, colleague, do they have pearls inside them? Yes? Then you should worry that your customers will break their teeth. Teeth are more precious than pearls when it comes to eating.' Eventually he found a stall where he was happy and started directing the stallholder as if he was making a movie.

'Yes, colleague, a kilo, but please: more panache when you weigh things. Take pride in your work. No, just a large handful of those. But do it with style, colleague, style is all.'

When he had everything he wanted there was the usual fight between him and Reid over who was to pay.

'Please, colleague, do not embarrass me in front of my countrymen. You can pay next time.'

He would always win because even if Reid succeeded in putting some money in his hand or his pocket, Medar would throw it to the ground and shout angrily. And the next tramp to come along would be a hundred schillings richer.

As they walked from the Naschmarkt up towards Reid's apartment, Feargal suddenly ducked into a supermarket and emerged with two bottles of wine in a plastic bag dangling from his hook. Reid took this to be an example of macabre bad taste, particularly when he noticed the frozen stare on Christa's face as she watched him, but Feargal did not seem to notice the effect he was making, or if he did he kept his thoughts to himself. As they continued on their way, Reid fell into step with him and asked about his first impressions of the city.

'It's very provincial, would you not say? And like toytown for grown-ups with the trams and the way everything's kept so clean.'

Masking his own annoyance, Reid said: 'Don't say to the Viennese that you think they're provincial. They're dead proud of their cultural scene. Skin you alive, friend.'

'Oh, the cultural scene seems fine enough, though it's very much geared to a paying audience. I prefer places where it's all on the streets, you know. Filters upwards. It's to be expected, I suppose, with the city being stuck out here in the middle of nowhere, though. It's bound to be bit isolated. You know that underground station near the café we were at – Karlsplatz? Christa was telling me how it's becoming a terrible place these days with the junkies and everything. But you must know yourself: compare that to bits of London, or Dublin even more, and Karlsplatz is paradise.'

'Biggest topic of conversation in town at the moment. The theory is that the authorities are allowing it so they can keep tabs on what's happening. If you look around you'll probably see more plain clothes cops from the drugs squad than you'll see addicts. They get a bit excited about things here, it's true. But it's also true that Vienna's crime rate is catching up with the rest of Europe.'

'Might not be such a bad thing, if I can say so. The place feels to me as if it could do with a new set of balls.'

Reid was taken aback and couldn't find words to reply.

'Oh, Christ, you have to be so careful what you say. I think the town's great, all right. It just isn't Dublin or London. No buzz, you know.'

Reid did not have to answer because they had arrived at his block.

Once they were inside Reid's apartment, Medar put on some music and then fetched four bottles of beer from the fridge. He is supremely capable of making himself at home wherever he is, but Reid was not offended. They had lived together for five years and still spent most of their time at each other's apartment. They were used to sharing everything. Christa put the food away in the kitchen and Reid opened the French windows onto the balcony. He took an ashtray out, put it on the table and cleared away some of the junk which was always lying around out there. Feargal remained in the sitting room, browsing through the titles in Reid's extensive book collection, occasionally pulling a volume from its shelf by slipping the tip of his hook into the top of the spine. Reid's collection was built up as a result of his work at the radio station where, in addition to preparing news stories, he was responsible for reviewing new titles from England and America. Books were sent to him free by the publishers upon request. He was also good friends with the owner of one of the English bookshops in town and obtained books from him at a discount. English editions are expensive in Vienna. Every wall in Reid's apartment had book-shelves, all full, from the ceiling to the floor, and he had even started storing paperbacks in the cellar, something he regretted, but which was easier than finding a new apartment. It was a source of some amusement to Medar that his friend's home was so different from his own and, particularly, that Reid's taste in music suited his apartment just as Medar's collection is so appropriate to the starkness of the decor of his place. Reid liked some cool jazz but for the most part he listened to a mix of reggae, punk and new wave bands from the late seventies, music which he grew up with in England and which, Medar says, would 'fuck anyone's head'. Medar had found some Santana, though, so he was happy.

Feargal came out onto the balcony and sat down with a copy of a book by William Burroughs.

'Burroughs claims that he shot his wife by accident, but I harbour a secret fantasy that he did it on purpose. For a start it would square with his sense of humour, but apart from anything I think he's an almighty romantic at heart. There's not a lot that's more romantic than shooting your wife in Mexico.'

'Sounds like your idea of romantic shares something with Medar's, friend. Perhaps the two of you should get together and make sweet music by moonlight on the banks of the Danube.'

'Feargal is correct, colleague. The romantic is always linked to violence, either against others or against the self, physical or mental.'

'Though you wouldn't describe shooting your wife as an archetypal romantic act, surely?'

'Remember that the archetypal romantic hero wouldn't necessarily conform to what most people think when they hear the word romantic, especially when you get into the more Gothic stuff. Even Werther was pretty violent in his own fashion. And for that matter take a look at the romantic writers – Byron and Shelley didn't live what you'd call peaceful lives, Reid.'

'So maybe that's how I could become a writer, Medar, if I shoot you.'

'You would have to write something first. Anyway, I'm not your wife and you'd probably miss because you are so useless a specimen.'

'Another beer, friend?'

Reid did not want to get into another argument with Medar, partly because his brain was still not in full working order – and was not likely to be all day – and partly because Feargal was beginning to disturb him. It seemed to Reid that for someone who was dependent upon the generosity of others for his food and a place to sleep, Feargal made few compromises. He was an unwelcome intrusion on their comfortable familiarity as a group. And in a flash of honesty, Reid confessed that Feargal's interest in Christa, so apparent in the way he spoke to her and watched her, was a threat to their friendship. Reid's relationship with Christa was not an overtly sexual one – though at one stage, early on, it had been. Their friendship was exclusive in that neither had steady partners. If such a relationship would have made Christa happy, Reid would not have been against it. But he had doubts about Feargal's integrity, doubted the respect he would have for Christa's friendships with any other men were he to become involved with her. When he went through to the kitchen she was still there, cleaning the oven.

'Reid, you're disgusting, you know.'

'It's the cleaning woman, she never does anything around here. C'mon, leave it.'

It turned out that Feargal had a habit of using lighted cigarettes as bookmarks when he wanted to say something or take a sip of his drink and when there was no ashtray within reach. It would have bothered Reid whichever book Feargal had been reading at the time, but at that moment he had on his lap a rare first English edition of a Günter Grass novel which had cost a great deal of money. Feargal asked: 'Would the two of you say you were happier living in Vienna than you were at home?'

'I suppose we wouldn't have stayed here otherwise, friend. We're as happy, at least; there are advantages and there are drawbacks. In the end it doesn't make much more difference to me than the fact that the bars open all night and the rents are cheaper here than they are in London.'

Reid was glancing nervously at the book while he answered Feargal, his eyes drawn almost against his will to the glowing tip of the cigarette as it moved ever closer to the book's top trim, the grey ash congealing around it. He was reluctant to say anything about it because, in theory at least, Medar and he shared an ambivalent attitude towards objects and to be too possessive was seen as a failing. It was an attitude which had developed out of circumstance. When Reid and Medar first came to Vienna they stayed in a room with two others in a youth hostel in the twentieth. After a week of searching they found the apartment which Medar continues to occupy. It was rented at the time and filled with old furniture which had been left behind by a series of previous tenants and, mostly in a symbolic gesture, they had thrown out or given away everything except the desk and the wooden cabinet which remain there to this day. They had come with few possessions of their own and did not wish to be weighed down by those of others they had never met.

Reid had been reading Régis Debray's *Revolution in the Revolution* at the time and, in a playful spirit, he and Medar chose to regard their early days in Vienna as a kind of an insurrection against the prevailing order which, as they saw it, sought to bar them from living in Austria. Medar's apartment thus became the *foco* base and they observed Debray's 'three golden rules' – 'Constant vigilance, constant mistrust, constant mobility.' They used pseudonyms and gave false addresses to people they met but did not like. Above all they recognized that with their relative lack of possessions they were at an advantage over others who came to Vienna seeking work, people who needed large apartments to house the things they had brought with them, the lifestyles they clung to. As Reid would often say: 'If you can't carry it, you don't need it.' That was their maxim.

The strategy had worked, if success can be measured in terms of money and friends, and neither Reid nor Medar was willing to relinquish those earlier ideals completely. For Reid, though, that had become little more than a convention at best, a philosophy he pretended to but did not in truth adhere to. Habits such as carrying his passport wherever he went were no more than meaningless legacies of a time when Medar and he might indeed have needed to leave everything behind and take a train to Germany or Italy and start afresh. They would have done it then – as Medar says, you can buy bread and cigarettes most places these days – but after seven years in a city the ability to leave behind a comfortable existence with all its accessories is lost. Reid was about to say something about the cigarette when Feargal took it from the book, drew swiftly on it once, and stubbed it out on the balcony floor. Reid suspected that it was a deliberate attempt to bait him because Feargal looked at him very calmly and smiled innocently before saying: 'Well, you've built up an impressive library, at least.'

'Say we go to this zoo, then?'

'Shall we visit Franz on the way? I did say to him that I'd probably go by, even just to say hello.'

'Do you have the car with you?'

'No, my brother has it. He's gone to Linz to see some friends for the day.'

'I wonder, colleagues, how would it be if we took Franz with us to the zoo?'

Christa and Reid looked at each other doubtfully. They had attempted to obtain permission to take Franz out before, but the nurses had always refused, saying that he was too frail. Reid could not imagine that Christa's adventure with him earlier in the week would make the situation any easier.

'I don't know how we'd fix it, friend. They're pretty tight in there.'

'We can at least speak with Franz about it. There is always the possibility that he will know a way to get out, perhaps avoiding the necessity of asking the nurses for their permission.'

'I'll bet he does, knowing Franz.'

'If you don't mind my asking, who is this man exactly anyway?'

'Franz Lasker. Oldest Jew in Vienna.'

'Great guy. Used to be a waiter in one of the coffee houses, until Hitler came. Then he took his family to New York, came back at the end of the occupation in fifty-five. You'll like him. He tells some good stories.'

'How old did you say he is?'

'Nearly a hundred. Though you wouldn't know it to talk to him, cunning sod.'

'To look at, though.'

'Yeah, to look at. Methuselah Senior, Franz is.'

'And how did you come to meet the man?'

'Reid here bought this place off him a couple of years back. We just kept in touch, that's all.'

'But if this home's so terrible why does he stay there? Could he not just move out?'

'It's not that simple, friend. My old neighbour was a Nazi, former camp guard. He hated Franz and had him committed, it's easily done. Of course Franz is fine and the shrinks at the hospital said so, but you know these social workers. Same the world over. They put him in the home "for his own good" or some such shit.'

'But that's like something out of the last century. Was there nothing could be done to stop it?'

'Old fashioned city, Vienna. The funny thing is that the Nazi got carted off a few months later, too. He was done three times in two weeks for trying to torch the synagogue. Crazy as hell, I tell you, he was lucky not to get shot with all the cops there.'

'It's a good way to get yourself a place to live, though. Find an apartment with some old guy living on his own, bribe the caretaker to tell the authorities he's senile and you're in, just like that.'

'You are joking, I hope, Christa.'

'It happens.'

'Let's go, yes?'

While Christa and Medar cleared the bottles away, Reid changed into some different clothes. He wished that he had felt up to taking a shower at Medar's before they had come out, but it would have to wait until they returned from the zoo. He smiled as one of Che Guevara's sayings came to mind: '. . . the hammocks of guerrilla fighters are known for their characteristic, individual odour.'

Feargal was still carrying Reid's copy of the Günter Grass novel in his hand as they were leaving so Reid said to him: 'Here, I'll get you a paperback of this, I have one somewhere. Then you can put it in your pocket instead of having to carry it.'

'Don't worry yourself. I'll probably not get around to reading it anyway. I hardly ever do unless they sit on the shelf staring at me for six months first, you know.'

He handed over the book and, as casually as he could, Reid placed it on the table inside the door before he locked up and followed everyone down the stairs.

They had all taken another bottle of beer each and Reid's mood improved: it felt good to be out in the street with the sun shining and beers in their hands, as if they were on holiday. The start of the summer in Vienna is worth celebrating after the winter when it is often too cold to have any real pleasure. This summer held more potential than ever for enjoyment because, with the events in Czechoslovakia and Hungary, the city was becoming even more cosmopolitan and for Reid it was this multicultural element which made Vienna a joy to live in. Franz's home was in the eighteenth district, so they would be making quite a detour on their way to the zoo. It was unimportant: Reid loved travelling by tram – so much less of a chore than journeys by underground. They could watch people on the streets and look out for friends or acquaintances doing something stupid when they did not know they were being watched.

If there was a shadow over Reid's enjoyment it was his growing resentment of Feargal's cynicism in his view of Vienna and its people. Vienna was, after all, Reid's home and he found Feargal's attitude towards it offensive. As far as Reid was concerned, if a city was clean and there was seldom any trouble on the streets, that was no reason to dismiss it as boring. Feargal had said that life in Vienna was not like 'real life' but he would not say what he meant by that. He was cynical again when he saw a motorist being stopped by the Environmental Police because his car exhaust was making too much noise.

'But it's good, Feargal. If you let people get away with things like that, the problems just get worse.'

'Surely, surely, but all this state control, Christa . . . Do you not think it removes some of the humanity from life?'

'Personally, colleague, I feel that it does. But within the structure of Austrian society there are many opportunities for spontaneity, because this structure allows economic freedom. The structure of Turkish society is, however, built on the hot-blooded mentality. As a result there is no economic freedom or political freedom and little real spontaneity. This is problematical. The Turkish system, although built in a more human way, is inhuman. Austrian society is the other way.'

'But surely there's plenty of people here lacking any economic freedom. This place might be pretty, but it's not utopia. You said yourself, Medar, that those men selling the newspapers earn a pittance for standing in the street fourteen hours a day, six days a week.'

Reid said: 'What you say is true, friend, but it's true of all countries to some extent. There are, for example, laws in England which simply couldn't exist here. There are laws here which do not exist – or are not enforced – in England. For my part I would rather have policemen stopping drivers from polluting the air than preventing citizens drinking between eleven at night and eleven in the morning in the place of their choice. When it comes down to it, in any case, the reason we stay here is because our friends are here. That's the most important thing, don't you think?'

'Yes, friends are important. But so is humanity in itself, as a quality. Well, I should talk. All I'm interested in is having the freedom for myself. It just occurs, that's all.'

'I think you do something about that just by being yourself.

Every time you laugh because you're happy you're bucking the system.'

'Reid has some strange ideas, colleague. Do not let them worry you.'

'We're here.'

The building where Franz lived was a new one, purpose built to house old people and to ensure that they could not go missing by accident or by design, so Reid knew it would never be easy to get the old man out. In the first place the nurse on duty at the reception desk was unhappy about the idea of allowing four visitors into the building when they had no appointment. Eventually Christa convinced her that they would not excite Franz and they were allowed to go through to the gardens where he was sitting in his wheelchair, on his own, staring into the distance looking miserable. Reid always marvelled at the expressiveness of Franz's features, at the deep lines etched into his skin. He brightened up when he saw them but, Reid thought, his greeting lacked the usual effusiveness and it was all too apparent that he was unhappy.

'Welcome, welcome. You did not tell me, Christa, that we would be having a party.'

'Franz, how would you like to come out with us for the day?'

'Of course, I should like to spend the day somewhere with you very much indeed, but as you know there are problems with these Nazi doctors and nurses.'

'Come on, Franz, they're only doing their jobs.'

'Following orders?'

'Is there some way we could smuggle you out? Got a back gate or something?'

Franz screwed up his eyes and closed them for a moment, then he smiled craftily.

'There is of course the fire alarm.'

'They let everyone out?'

'Indeed. We are supposed to assemble here, in the gardens, but anyone who is in the front part of the building, in reception or near one of the fire exits on that side, should go into the street and wait there to be collected by the staff. If three of you took me to reception, perhaps to ask some foolish question, the other could set off the fire alarm and we might attempt our escape. How does that sound?'

'Sounds fine to me. Who's going to do what?'

'I'll set off the alarm. If I get caught I can't get into as much trouble as you people. Do you know where I'd find one, Mr Lasker?'

'If you go up the stairs, turn right and go to the end of the corridor you will find an emergency exit which leads directly to the street. When you open the doors the alarm is set off automatically, but you must run and hide somewhere because there is an office at the foot of the stairs and you may be seen.'

'Feargal, I'll come with you and then we can all arrange to meet up . . . where, guys?'

'Medar, your place? It's not so far.'

'We can, in any case, take a taxi.'

When they had sorted out the final details, Medar and Reid wheeled Franz through into the reception area while Feargal and Christa went upstairs. Just as the nurse was explaining to Reid why it was 'strictly forbidden' to take alcohol into the home, the alarm sounded and they were hurried out into the street along with a dozen other inmates and their visitors. After ten minutes or so two fire engines arrived and a crowd of passers-by gathered to see what was happening, so they drifted away round a corner and hailed a taxi.

'So, Franz, we made it. You're free for the day.'

'Indeed. But there will be problems later.'

'Later is later. Maybe you should not return to the home. Stay here with me, or at Reid's. You are welcome.'

'There are advantages to staying in the home which would not apply were I living here as your guest, Medar. I can take care of the nurses. It is simply a matter of behaving as they expect you to – very stupid, that is. They are seduced by their youthfulness and believe it to signify superiority over their charges. In truth they are fools. Typical Austrians. I should call them to inform them that I am at least alive and not dead or the problems will be all the greater. May I borrow your telephone?'

While the old man called the home Reid opened the door for Christa and Feargal who had just arrived. They were still laughing about their adventures and Reid felt a jar of anger when he saw them.

'Can you believe it, Reid, we got caught.'

'It wasn't a problem, though. I kept my mouth shut and Feargal pretended he couldn't speak German. He gave them a false name and an address in Ireland. They weren't so bad about it.'

'Did you have any problems with Franz?'

'No, no problems. You see the crowd?'

'They like their spectator sports, the Viennese, do they not?'

'Seriously, though. They all gather at a moment's notice in the street and talk to each other about whatever's going on. We're strange people, I told you.'

'I like that, though. It's not what you'd expect in a city like this, complete strangers yapping on to each other about nothing at all.'

'You should see them at election time or when everything was blowing up in Hungary and Czechoslovakia. They just talk shit the whole time, though. Is Franz OK?'

'Sure, he's just calling the home now to try and calm them down about it. Don't know what he'll say to them, but you know Franz.'

*

Franz told the nurses that he had completely forgotten that he lived in the home and, thinking that he was lost, had taken a taxi back to his old address – Reid's apartment. He would return as soon as he could, but he was lost again, so he was not sure what time that would be. Reid was silent while Franz related this and while Christa explained what they had planned for the day. She and Feargal seemed so at ease with each other that he felt excluded, as if he were the newcomer, not the Irishman. Reid's affair with Christa had been short-lived. One night, soon after they first met each other, they had dinner together – Medar had been out for the evening – and for reasons Reid still did not understand they had ended up in bed. It was her first time and, in fact, her only time as far as Reid was aware. The repercussions of the event went on for many weeks: a series of terse phonecalls in which she informed him that she had not had her period, that she was sure she was pregnant, that she hated him. The calls culminated in her arrival at the Ottakringerstrasse apartment one day, a pregnancy testing kit in her bag. She could not use it at home, she said, because her mother might interrupt her. Could she use it here? That had been four months after their night together and with disbelief Reid had agreed. They spent a perverse thirty minutes together awaiting the outcome which was inconclusive. Her period had started that evening and they had remained close ever since, but with the subtlest sexual tension between them. To Reid it was clear that any change in the nature of that tension was bound to change the relationship.

'The zoo, why, I haven't been to the zoo in sixty years. More, even. Terrible place.'

'Shall we go there, then?'

'Of course, of course. But first, if you do not mind indulging an old man, I should like a coffee.'

Christa rolled her eyes and went through to the kitchen to make some.

'And Medar, you would perhaps do me the honour of packing that pipe there for me, if you have no objection to my borrowing it.'

'Of course not. I have not smoked it for several years, but it should be fine.'

'It is a good pipe, Dunhill is good. Why do you not smoke it any more?'

'When I was younger such things pleased me. Perhaps one day I shall start again. The tobacco, anyway, is fresh. A gift from a friend who visited from Turkey recently.'

Christa brought a coffee through for each of them and they watched Franz's face relax into a picture of contentment as he sipped from the cup and lit the pipe.

'You I do not know, or . . . ?'

'Franz Lasker, Feargal . . .'

'O'Neill. From Ireland and the rest of the world.'

'Irish . . . Then you too are part of a great cultural diaspora such as my people.'

'For sure, Mr Lasker. The Gael and the Jew have plenty in common, it's a fact.'

'Both share a history which is honourable and dishonourable, tragic and facile. Interestingly it is the honourable which has been facile and the dishonourable which has been tragic. One might expect otherwise. Welcome to Vienna, friend, but please, you will call me Franz. Only the nurses in the home call me Mr Lasker in their ignorance.'

'Franz is a doctor.'

'A doctor? And I'd been told you worked as a waiter all your life.'

'Doctor of Philosophy, honorary, from the University of Vienna. It is one of those absurdities which seem to please the Viennese when they have stuffed themselves too full of pork to eat any more and their coffee has gone cold in its cup. "Ah, yes," they say, "let us make amends. Franz Lasker is very old and furthermore he is Jewish . . . He shall be a Doctor of Philosophy and by this mark of respect we are absolved of our guilt . . ." Fools.'

'Franz isn't too keen on the Viennese.'

'With the exception of those present, of course. Were you aware, Feargal, that despite the fact that Austrians comprised only eight per cent or so of the population of Hitler's Germany, half of the Jews who died in the Shoah were killed upon the instructions of Austrian Death Camp commandants: Stangl, Fritsch, Gerbing, Burger, Seidl, Globocnik, Sommern-Frankenegg, Murer, Roschmann, above all Eichmann himself. And we should not forget Hitler. In Vienna Hitler found his inspiration before the first war. Indeed, the Habsburgs will be called to account for much which grew out of their empire. Did you know that they funded the Bolsheviks? They wanted to destabilize Russia's monarchy, so they helped Trotsky print his papers. Stalin too spent time here. Lenin was in Czechoslovakia. Think of it: in the first fourteen years of this century the seeds were sown for the annihilation of how many people? Fifty million? One hundred million? Two hundred million? Untold suffering as a result of several centuries of unremarkable incest. My apologies, I could go on at some length.'

'Please do. I'm fascinated.'

'Though if we don't leave soon the zoo will be closed. Franz talks history at length wherever he is, friend. You'll get your lesson.'

'Quite right, Reid. The zoo is as good a place for history lessons as anywhere. Let us go there.'

They decided to take a taxi to the zoo because Franz's wheelchair would have been too much of a problem on the trams. When they arrived at Schönbrunn Feargal seemed impressed for the first time all day.

'Makes the Brits' efforts seem a little sad by comparison, does it not?'

'Indeed, colleague, but consider the hardship which must have been caused by the building of this.'

'Medar's right. All the tourist guides go on about this place, but if you think about it this is more a symbol of social philistinism than of artistic beauty.'

'Count the bricks and for every one of them a Jew was murdered.'

93

'Is that a fact?'

'Do not take Franz too literally, colleague. He has a fine sense of injustice and of allegory and an enduring contempt for symbols of power be they nurses' uniforms, this building or the Westautobahn which Hitler built. But his use of facts and figures is at best symbolic.'

'For a philosopher, Medar, your disregard for semiology is regrettable. For a Turk it is unforgivable.'

'The dialectic is nevertheless of some interest.'

There was a long queue for tickets to go into the zoo and when Reid saw that the ticket collector had left his post he tugged at Christa's sleeve and whispered to her and the others that they should simply walk through. As they were passing the barrier he heard a shout from someone waiting in the queue. When he looked back he saw that the man who had shouted and his friend were trying to do the same thing. They hesitated at the barrier and were caught by the ticket collector who went running over to them. They pointed at Reid and the others, but the attendant simply glanced over and shrugged. Some succeed, others fail. It is all a game.

The zoo was built in the latter part of the nineteenth century and in architectural terms it is attractive. It was designed as a showpiece for a world fair, and matches the palace. In its time it was probably regarded as a magnificent zoological achievement, but by today's standards and especially in comparison to modern zoos in other cities, it seems cruel and inhumane. Their first stop was the cages where the big cats are kept – some lions and then some beautiful black panthers. None of them spoke while they looked at the panthers and Reid reflected that, no matter how many times one had seen this before, the size of the cages was always a shock. Franz was the first to speak.

' "Sein Blick ist vom Vorübergehn der Stäbe/ so müd geworden, daß er nichts mehr hält./ Ihm ist als ob es tausend Stäbe gäbe/ und hinter tausend Stäben keine Welt." Rilke.'

'You'd think they'd have done something about this by now.'

'You know what we were saying, about romanticism and violence: I think this zoo is a good example. This is a very romantic place in some respects, and certainly in its time I'd imagine it was seen as romantic, but there's a violence all around us. Not just the size of the cages, but those hunks of meat they're feeding the animals in there, everything about it. Of course maybe for someone who's sensitive to the suffering of these creatures, the violence is too blatant – you know, those panthers just look miserable and you don't need to be a vegetarian to see that. But a hundred years ago that violence still existed and this would have been considered romantic. It's our attitudes to violence that have changed, not the idea of the romantic. I think if the violence is too overt the romance is lost. The place should be beautiful and the violence subtle in relationship to our perceptions of it.'

'Essentially you are correct, colleague, but for one thing: this is Austria and, as Franz will detail at length, the Austrians have a violent heritage which they do not relinquish willingly. Look around you: for the Austrians here this remains a romantic place. That, Reid, is why nothing has been done about this.'

'Medar is right. You need only stand near a sausage stand for half an hour to see something of the Austrian attitude towards animals.'

'Tell me, friend, do you approve of the romantic? As you define it, I mean. Does this type of violence please you?'

'I'm not sure that I'd want to answer that one, Reid. It might be an unromantic thing to do. As I said, or Medar said, the romantic is inextricably bound up with the violent, but for the romantic person the violence of his deeds or his surroundings has to be barely visible even to himself, it has to be wrapped up in his desires so that the violence, in so far as it can be detected, must be an integral part of the romanticism, not something external to it.'

'What do you think, Franz? Was the Holocaust romantic?'

'Come on, Reid, I'm saying that the romantic is always violent, not that the violent is always romantic.'

'Franz?'

'Unfortunately, Reid, I believe that there is some truth in what Feargal says. I trust that I have seen enough in my life to be able to reject quite emphatically anything romantic, and it is true that violence in itself can never be said to be romantic. I suspect that it is the actual process of cloaking violence in one's desires which assigns the violence its romantic appeal. For some of my people, who desire that they be seen as the chosen people, the violence of the Holocaust has indeed acquired a romantic element. Perhaps in the years immediately succeeding the war this was not the case. As Feargal says, the violence was too near, too overt. But as time passed the romance was born. Tales of heroism in the camps, in the Warsaw Ghetto, stories about Wiesenthal hunting Nazis in South America . . . All these things became tied up with the desires of the Jews after the war to assert their status in the world. The cause, the Holocaust, achieved a status in turn which in my view it does not deserve. They worship Wiesenthal, but in rational terms he simply plays his part in a greater tragedy about which there should be nothing romantic. This is not true of all Jews, of course, but of some. It is the victims who are today's romantic heroes: the blacks in South Africa, the Irish, the Palestinians. Particularly so in the eyes of well to do whites in their comfortable homes in Grinsing, shielded as they are from the realities of the violence they see and hear about on their television sets.'

'So you don't condone that, Franz.'

'No, Christa, I do not condone it, I do not condemn it. It simply is so.'

'Though you'd approve more of the classical than the romantic from what you're saying.'

'Certainly not, Feargal. The classical has a violence all its own in which I have every bit as little interest.'

'So what, then, Franz?'

'There is an old Jewish saying: If you are offered two choices, take the third.'

'And that would be?'

'You ask me, Medar? You surprise me.'

'Nevertheless, I am interested to hear what you have to say.'

'If both the romantic and the classical share a propensity to violence, and if this violence is found to be unacceptable, then we must ask ourselves what is non-violent and, indeed, whether non-violence is at all possible in the modern world.'

'But what do you think?'

'Me, I am altogether too modern for my own good.'

'So your third option is no option at all.'

'No, indeed not. My option is simply to listen to jazz music for most of my waking hours and to adhere to the arcane principles of non-action as far as is possible.'

'Now I know you are winding me up, Franz.'

His face crinkled into a grin and he nodded vigorously before returning his attention to the panther which had stopped its pacing and was lying down, licking its paws.

By the time they reached the seals it was almost feeding time and a large crowd had gathered on the tiered viewing area. For all their perceived faults the Viennese show respect for the old and handicapped and whilst the others stood at the back, mothers and fathers pulled their children out of the way and Reid was permitted to wheel Franz down to the front. They would get wet, he knew, but Franz had insisted that there was nothing in the zoo he wanted to see more than the seals being fed. While they were waiting for the zookeeper to come with his buckets of fish Franz said to Reid: 'Feargal disturbs you, no?'

Reid was surprised that it showed and said so. Franz was quiet for a moment and they watched the old bull seal playing and splashing the crowd – fully aware that it was the star of the show for the moment. Then he said:

'It doesn't show at all, but I know you well enough, Reid. He disturbs me slightly too, though I suspect that I understand him better than you do, and in any case I am not intimidated, as you are, by his lack of a hand. You should not be either, because the hook suggests that he does not take himself as seriously as one might initially imagine. Well, it is many years since I was his age, but only a few for you. You are too similar to him, you need to fear him in some way, perhaps, or at least be aware of the threat he poses to you. He challenges you, Reid. No one likes that.'

'You truly think we're similar?'

'Reid, do you not remember how you told me that you modelled yourself on the great revolutionaries when you were younger? Guevara, Makhno, Durruti? Surely you would acknowledge the existence of a romantic streak to your own character. And don't forget that your revolutionaries were hardly pacifists.'

'I suppose. But somehow there seemed to be a point to what those people did. They weren't doing it just to be romantic. It seems to me that Feargal, with this Gothic image he cultivates and what he says about violence, wants the romantic to be an end in itself. For Guevara and the others wasn't the romance just a by-product of the aims they had?'

'Was there ever a point to what you did? Oh, by all means, the words you spoke were honourable enough, but in truth did you ever do anything other than romanticize yourself and your life and then go on to exploit the image that others had of you for your own purposes, for the purpose of gaining the very power and wealth which you scorned so vocally?'

'I make no excuses for that, but my beliefs have changed.'

'What changed first? Your beliefs or your circumstances? Did you adapt your circumstances to your beliefs? At first, perhaps, but later you altered your beliefs to suit your circumstances. It is not an uncommon phenomenon. Indeed, I have seen it and experienced it myself. I told you, did I not, that I was associated with the workers who took over the Karl-Marx-Hof in '34. People change, but we must look for the reasons. I am not criticizing you, Reid, because there are arguments to support your way of life which, in terms of logic at least, do not differ from any other arguments. The logic of fascism is not substantially different from the logic of communism, anarchism or liberalism. Each of them results in wholesale slaughter. Indeed, fascism could be said to have a certain practical honesty which the others lack. I simply suggest that if Feargal disturbs you, it is to yourself that you must look for answers, not to him.'

'I don't understand how you of all people can say that, Franz, about fascism.'

'With ease. Austria is a social democracy of a relatively high order as Europe goes. But by its very nature there are subtle stresses at work in Austrian society which kill every bit as efficiently as the gas chambers ever did. Furthermore, if you speak to someone who, for example, left Germany for Poland before the war began, as a great many did, they might well tell you that the months in Poland, free from routine and filled with adventure as they were, were exciting and fulfilling where a peaceful existence in Germany was not. This should not be a revelation to you, Reid. Life attains a certain expediency under such conditions which, all too often, it lacks otherwise. People in Austria today do not die in gas chambers or of starvation in a concentration camp, but of boredom, of an awareness of their very peaceful insignificance. Hence the romance of violence, Reid.'

'That's a pretty depressing way to see the world, Franz. I'd never realized you did.'

'Perhaps I do, perhaps not. If there are things which come with age, one of them is the ability to open one's mind to such possibilities. That is something which you will learn before too long, I suspect.'

The zookeeper arrived and started feeding the seals so they did not speak again until the show was over, Franz watching the action excitedly and clapping whenever the bull seal caught a fish that was thrown its way. Reid soon lost interest and started watching the other people who were around them, young parents and their children mostly, innocently enjoying their day out. For them, he thought, this probably was romantic, but the crowd made him feel claustrophobic and all he wanted to do was to get out and go for a beer to get rid of his hangover.

'You know how the Viennese keep going on about how the suicide rate here's higher than anywhere else? I was reading an article the other day which said Austria's only fifth in Europe, after Hungary, Finland, Switzerland and Denmark.'

'But what about the figures for the individual cities? I think maybe there are more here than in any other city.'

'I don't know.'

'You know nothing, colleague.'

'Cut the crap, Medar.'

They were sitting beneath the Gloriette, looking down towards the palace. They had become bored of the zoo and after the seals were fed they had decided to leave. Reid had not really enjoyed the visit because it seemed to him that the zoo became worse every time he went, even though they were trying to promote and improve it and build bigger compounds for the animals. He asked Feargal: 'So, what does the zoo tell you about Vienna or the Viennese, friend?'

He'd been quiet since they had come out and he lit up a cigarette before he answered. He and Medar were two of a kind that way.

'I wouldn't want to be too hasty about passing judgement if the truth be told. Let's just say that from what I've seen of Vienna, the zoo fits the city pretty well.'

'Franz?'

'In so far as the Viennese are an utterly barbaric people and the zoo succeeds in being emblematic of that barbarism, I think Feargal is correct. For the rest I have nothing to say.'

'And what does Christa have to say about all this, us passing comment on her city and her people?'

'Christa thinks nothing. You see that poster at Reid's place? "My fatherland is international." I don't give a damn, say what you like.'

'What time is it now, Medar?'

'Perhaps time to return to your apartment, eat some food. It is too early for dinner and too late for lunch, but nevertheless . . .'

'Franz?'

'I wonder if you would help me find a taxi and I shall return to the home. I am tired now.'

'Are you sure, Franz? My offer was a serious one: you are welcome to stay at my apartment for as long as you like.'

'Thank you, Medar, but as I said: there are certain advantages to life in the home, not least the fact that there is an elevator to take me from one floor to the next. You would soon tire of carrying me up and down your stairs. I hope, however, that we can repeat these adventures another time. I should like very much to visit the Prater. It has been many years since I was there.'

They wheeled Franz down the hill and over the courtyard to the front entrance and saw him into a taxi. Then the four of them went to the underground station and rode back to Kettenbrucken-gasse and walked to Reid's apartment. Ian, his guest from Australia, was there when they arrived, listening to music out on the balcony. He was a friendly person but he was nervous about taking up too much space, especially when Reid had guests round. Reid had told him not to concern himself, but as soon as they went in he disappeared off to his room and five minutes later he went out. Medar took control of the cooking and Christa helped him while Feargal and Reid went out onto the balcony with some more beers.

'How did you lose your hand? If you don't mind my asking.'

Feargal paused to light a cigarette and drew on it a couple of times before he replied.

'When I was a small boy in Cork and I still didn't know what others meant when they said the world was round, I imagined somehow a little piece of string which I could twist around my finger, coiling it tighter and tighter until my skin went red, then blue and cold and I'd untwine the string and there'd be an imprint there in my flesh, white weals which I could press so they'd sting. A funny way to see the world, do you not think, Reid?'

'Children always have fantasies like that, ways of trying to understand the things they hear.'

'Yes, Reid, that's true. But you know, that image stayed with me, I never let it go the way people normally do as they grow older. The way I see it, it was as if that little piece of string crept off into some dark recess of my mind and stayed there, coiling and uncoiling like a black snake, restless and awaiting the fullness of the day when it would come forth.'

'And did it?'

'Well, that's why I've no hand, you see. It's a bit of a story, but to cut it short, when I was fifteen I was a heroin addict. It's a funny thing, but heroin generates an awful dark humour in you at times and as a joke – as a joke, mind – I had a tattoo put on me. It was of a little black snake uncoiling from the back of my hand and striking the length of my forefinger. It was a work of art, Reid, a true work of art. It had red eyes either side of the top joint and little fangs hanging down under the nail and a little red tongue on the end of my finger. You could see every scale on the thing. Cost me an arm and a leg to get it done. If you see what I mean.'

'So what happened to it?'

He held up his left hand, palm facing Reid, to tell him to let him go on.

'You know what they say, Reid: there are no snakes in Ireland. If I'm honest my little joke didn't go down too well with anyone in the town. Not just with my parents, but with my friends as well. Heroin was just a hobby for most of them, you know. A weekend thing. I was too keen on the stuff for their liking and I had to leave. I went to Dublin thinking I could start all over, or at least find some people who were my sort. That didn't work out either because I got caught and stuck in this young offenders place run by the church. Godawful it was, but it got me off the junk for a while until I escaped and went to London. That's where I did this. With an axe. Don't ask me why, Reid. Perhaps because one of their sermons said if your hand causes you to sin, cut it off. Maybe because I really did want to get off the stuff, you know. Maybe because of that damned tattoo, I just wanted to get rid of it.'

'And did you get off it?'

'Too right. I was in hospital for two weeks. Trauma, you know. So after that I never went back on it. Left London, been travelling around ever since.'

'And now, what do you think now?'

'I never learnt to write with my left hand, or do anything at all complicated, though it's going on four years now. That's why the notion of writing poetry appeals. Less words to put down. But as well as that there's always the fear I'd start on the stuff again if I had a hand to do it with. I don't want that, Reid. More than anything at all I don't want that.'

'So that's why you don't settle as well.'

'Yes, one reason I travel is so I don't have to learn to use this. You can do without a hand when you're travelling. It doesn't take much to open a train door or to stick your thumb out for a lift. And the bar I worked at, this was a feature.'

'And poetry? You really want to write poetry?'

'I don't know. Maybe I like the idea of being a poet more than I'd like the practice of it. A romantic occupation it would be, surely. As you'd say, Reid, the issue is an . . . academic one? At the minute, anyway.'

Just then Christa came out onto the balcony with some more

beers for them. Feargal was staring at Reid and smiling as he took the beer and handed her a cigarette.

'What's he cooking?'

'I don't know but in Turkish it's called "split stomach". Smells good, if that helps.'

'Leave him to me, yeah?'

She took a seat and asked Feargal: 'Well?'

'Whatever Reid says, I think Vienna has the right amount of violence in its romance for me. I'll stick around a while. Reid's going to teach me to write properly with my left hand.'

'Are you a romantic, Feargal? By your own definition of the word?'

'One tries, Christa. One tries one's best. Narcissus is my middle name. Franz said something interesting earlier, that he didn't endorse either the classical or the romantic view because they share the same violence and that's what he rejects. Now I think that's interesting and fair enough if you want to believe in his third option, but there's still a difference between the two: the classical demands formal beauty, so in terms of a life it asks that your existence when seen as a whole be formally perfect. The romantic view is much more the human one: there it's the beauty of deeds alone that counts; it allows redemption for past errors by a redefinition of the context through further deeds. I couldn't possibly take a classical view – I condemned myself to the romantic many years ago just by not knowing what it was. The way I see it I might as well carry on by doing things properly.'

'Reid, do you understand what this guy's going on about? Because if you do I'm going back to the kitchen.'

'I'm interested.'

'You see, Reid, there's an inevitable incompleteness about a romantic life which can't exist with the classical. The romantic is driven by desire, the classical by moderation. If you desire more than you have, your life can never be called complete. That's something which I choose to celebrate, myself, and when I die, I want to die a violent death. I don't give a damn what the two of them said about it: Sartre was on the side of the classical, Camus the romantic.'

'Camus might not have agreed.'

'As I said, I don't give a damn what they thought: you read *The Outsider* and the inevitability of Camus' early death is staring you in the face. The man didn't want to die of old age any more than Sartre wanted his heaven to be a solitary confinement block.'

Reid did not answer because Camus was one of his favourite writers and, although he could see what point Feargal was seeking to make, he had always thought that it was a tragedy Camus had not lived longer. They sat without talking until Medar arrived with the food.

'So then, Medar, did you enjoy your trip to see the peculiar creatures?'

'The ancient Romans would have put two white balls in a jar
today, Feargal.'

Feargal laughed – the only one of them who had not heard
Medar's favourite line – and said: 'Back home they'd call that an
awful waste of a good jar of drink, Medar.'

'But, colleague, no more of a waste than if they only put one
ball in.'

'True, but if they put any balls in their drinks at all they'd have
regretted the action that much they'd have to put in three black
balls, four even, by way of penance for their deeds.'

'Unless they were Stoics, colleague.'

'In which case doubtless they'd have been wise enough not to
go wasting good booze in the first place.'

'Reid, you know what these assholes are on?'

Medar and Feargal launched into an explanation for Christa's
benefit but Reid had lost interest and anyway, the food was worth
concentrating on. Medar is an excellent cook and Reid would often
get him to cater if he wanted to give a dinner party or even simply
to have friends round for an evening of drinking and talking.
Medar's 'split stomach' was aubergines stuffed with minced meat
and tomato and spiced with cumin, all served with couscous and
a tomato salad. They drank the wine which Feargal had bought
earlier – it was not very good but there was lots of it and it
reminded Reid of when he first lived with Medar and they would
drink two litres of the worst red wine they could find every night
before they went out – to 'find their heads' as Medar puts it. One
becomes accustomed to drinking wine which is of a good quality,
but the occasional bottle of bad stuff pleased them, if only for
reasons of nostalgia, and as they drank it Medar would say, as he

did before: 'Only the worst is good enough for us, colleague. Only the worst will do.'

After the meal Christa and Reid cleared everything away and put the plates and pans in the dishwasher. As usual when Medar cooks, the kitchen was a disaster area and there was a lot of clearing up to do. Reid told Christa to leave it to him and go back out onto the balcony because he felt he needed a few minutes to himself. Somehow the hangover had become worse, probably with the sun and the bad wine and, even though he had taken a couple of aspirins, he had a headache which was stopping him from laughing and playing around with the others or joining in the conversation. He did little clearing up in the end and decided instead to take a shower which he thought might help. He felt better afterwards and put on another change of clothes because it was going to be cold in the evening.

The others had come in from the balcony and they were talking about what they could do the next day.

'Any ideas, Reid? Medar thought maybe the three of you could take me round Mauthausen or something. Christa could drive there.'

'Don't, please, friend. Or at least I think I'll give it a miss. If the zoo's barbaric I don't think there's a word in any language for that place. Once is enough for anyone's lifetime.'

'I remember when I went there, when I was fifteen or so on a school trip. We all had to go, you know, and on the bus everyone was really nervous so they kept making all sorts of jokes about Jews and ashtrays and things. I think that's too young to see it, actually, so I'd quite like to go again.'

'What does Franz think about it really, though. I know he keeps on about the Austrians, but why's he here?'

'Franz stays for the sake of annoying the Austrians, friends. He loved winding up my old neighbour, saying "Shalom" every time he saw him on the stairs or in the lift and giving him Ephraim Kischon books for Christmas. He's pretty outrageous at times. You should hear the things he says to the nurses – what was it today?'

' "Did your father gas my mother?" I think.'

'Yes, or "Is that my uncle's gold filling you're wearing for a wedding ring?" '

'And you had me feeling sorry for the man.'

'He knows how to get to them, it's true. So, shall we make a move, go somewhere?'

'By all means, colleague, but there is the question of where. I would suggest that we drink another beer while we decide.'

'I'll get them, you can start talking about it.'

'We haven't been to Miles Smiles in a while.'

Miles Smiles is a tiny jazz bar in the eighth which they all liked to go to, but because it is so small it is often difficult to get seats. It was still early, though.

They decided to walk because it was not so far from Reid's place. Feargal took his hook off on the way and Christa was carrying it which made Reid's stomach turn. When they arrived the bar was already quite full, but there was one table free and they sat down and ordered some drinks. While they were waiting Feargal said to Reid: 'Christa told me something of what you do, Reid. Do you not find it a crashing bore?'

'Not at all. It's fairly simple work and it's well paid.'

'Do you actually get to go on air?'

'Once a week to review books and plays.'

'Well, I suppose that's not so bad, but you must have to work long hours, even if it is easy.'

'Sure, but as I say, I get paid for it. It suits me. I have my apartment, I eat out all the time, I take good holidays. It's a fair life.'

'Medar would seem to me to have the right idea with this thing he does, at the refugee centre. Enough money to live on and drink, plenty of free time, a roof over his head. I don't see that you need any more than that.'

Reid shrugged because he did not see that it was any of Feargal's business anyway. Then Feargal said: 'I've always felt, myself, that the less you worry yourself about possessions the better your life gets to be.'

'I don't think I feel any different to you that way, Feargal. If I didn't enjoy my life I'd change it.'

Feargal just nodded and smiled.

When their drinks came Feargal asked: 'Would any of you care to join me in a smoke?'

There was a time when Reid would never have turned down the offer but by now there was more to lose if he was caught. Medar never touches dope because if he was sent back to Turkey he would be imprisoned immediately. While Medar and he shook their heads Christa shrugged in a noncommittal gesture of assent. Feargal went ahead and lit the ready-rolled joint he had taken from his pocket. He offered it firstly to Reid and then to Medar and Reid explained to him that it was too risky for them. Really it would be better if Feargal went outside to smoke it. He asked Christa if she wanted to go with him but she said no, she wasn't in the mood, so he went out on his own.

'Just like you some years ago, colleague.'

'But never in a bar, surely.'

'Possibly not, but on your first day in Vienna in a room in a youth hostel where even smoking cigarettes was prohibited.'

'One learns.'

'That is certainly true. With this beard you are truly looking ripe, colleague.'

'If I'm looking ripe I really don't know what that makes you, my man.'

'Riper, colleague. Much riper.'

'So, what do you guys think of him?'

Reid shifted in his seat somewhat uncomfortably but Medar said: 'Feargal is good. Young, a little immature, but good. We must make sure he stays some time here, Christa. If there were not these problems I would have liked to smoke with him, out of courtesy at least.'

'Oh, I think he'll stick around a while. He asked me on the way here if it was really OK for him to stay at my place. He wants to learn to write with his left hand, he says, then take it from there.'

After a few minutes Feargal returned.

'You know, my grandmother was a fearsome old cow. Used to tell us a story, my brother and I. Well, not a story exactly, but sort of a story: "If God breathes on you and you're good," she'd say, "a little glow of warmth will kindle in your heart and spread through your body until your whole soul is aflame with love. But if God breathes on you and you're found to be bad, your soul will turn firstly to ice, then to stone and, after a long, long time, it'll crumble to dust and be scattered by the wind." By Christ she was a dreary old cow, but she could put the fear of God in a child when it suited her, you know.'

He had gone white as a sheet and he stopped abruptly. Christa asked him if he was all right and Medar said: 'Colleague, you should not use these drugs if this is their effect on you.'

'Medar, don't start, OK. Feargal, do you want to go outside again, get some fresh air?'

He nodded and Christa helped him to his feet and out the door.

When Christa came back she was laughing.

'He's really ill. I put him in a taxi and sent him home. I hope he's OK – the taxi driver made me give him two hundred schillings in case he's sick.'

Reid felt relieved that Feargal had gone. He had felt under attack all day. The fact that Feargal would be staying in Vienna for longer was a blow, but although he usually saw Christa quite often he did not depend on her company as much as he did on Medar's. If their friendship was affected it would be a loss to him, but he felt that it was something he could resign himself to. In any case, Reid was by no means convinced that Feargal was the type to stay in one place and he did not imagine that Vienna would appeal to his taste in the long run.

Medar seemed more relaxed as well, but Christa was restless and quiet. After another drink she said she wanted to go home and see Feargal because she was worried that he might be ill after smoking the whole joint himself. Medar and Reid said they would go with her and then maybe on to somewhere else, somewhere in the centre for a change.

Her apartment was on the edge of the first district, close to the University, so they walked. They said little. It seemed to Reid as if conversation had become superfluous without Feargal's presence. Perhaps it was simply because the whole day had been for his benefit and now that the audience had left half-way through the show they all felt at a loss for words. When they reached the Ring, Medar said he wanted to go home because it had been a long day and he was tired. Reid suspected that he would probably go and visit his whore because he had plenty of money that he had not spent on drinks and it would be unlike him to save it. Reid reluctantly decided to walk Christa back to her place and then he too would go home, or somewhere else.

Feargal had made it back to Christa's apartment without any problems. He was sitting at the table in the dining room, back to the window, a pen in his hand and a notebook in front of him, carefully forming letters and words on the paper. When they walked in he looked up with a smile and said: 'You missed me, then. I'm just in the middle of practising my joined-up. It's coming quite easily so perhaps poetry's not the only option after all, Reid. It's like being back at school, though.'

Christa went across to him and leaned over his shoulder to look at what he'd written.

'Feargal, that's great. I can read it, at least.'

'I'm pleased to hear it. It's taken me the best part of an hour.'

'I'm going to buy you a typewriter. Won't that be easier?'

'A typewriter? Well, we'll see. I'm quite enjoying doing this after my own left-handed fashion if you see what I . . .'

Reid closed the door quietly behind him as he stepped out into the hallway and went down the stairs, into the street. When he looked up Christa and Feargal were silhouetted in the window. He was holding his hook to her face, tracing the outline of her lips with its tip as they looked at each other.

Reid watched them for a few moments before starting the twenty-minute walk to his home, aware that the subtlest of shifts had taken place in the fabric of his universe, aware too that nothing he could do would change that. The wind was up and he shivered slightly, but in his heart he thought he could feel a glow of warmth and he smiled. Tomorrow he would give Feargal that Günter Grass book.

There were rules

There were rules, of course. Rigorously defined and to be strictly followed. The laws of self-interest policed the game without need for external arbiters. It was an agreement made in a world where social conventions could not participate. And they had stuck to it. George alone knew her as Adele. Her mother's name. To everyone else, and to him when they were in public, she was Monika. He was permitted to tell his friends – their friends – about their experiences together, but he was not allowed to refer the stories to the Monika they knew. Adele existed on the periphery of their understanding, though she was often central to their thoughts. The mystery of her identity intrigued them, enticed them, seduced them.

The form was always broadly the same: Adele would go to Harry Lime's, the bar which George owned on the Neubaugürtel, by the Westbahnhof, and sit there alone, drinking a coffee and reading a copy of the *International Herald Tribune*, something she never did otherwise. This was the signal for him to meet her the following day at the time and place they had arranged on their last meeting. In theory, by bringing her a glass of mineral water, George could indicate that he was unable to come. He never had, however. He was obsessive in this respect. It was impossible for him to refuse to meet her. Out of fear, she supposed, that it might upset her and prejudice the future of the affair. This despite her repeated emphasis that he was not obliged to come at her convenience. Adele was aware that she had the upper hand in the relationship, though she asked only for equality and mutuality.

When she picked him up in her car she would blindfold him and drive him to the street where she lived, taking as roundabout a route as possible. This was not because she distrusted him, but because she felt that if he knew his precise location in the city it would undermine his concentration on the work to hand. It was important, too, that he trust her completely when he was with her. Just as she trusted him when he was back in his bar with their other friends. It was their shared vulnerability which was of prime importance to the success of the venture.

When they reached her block she would take him, still blind-folded, into the courtyard and up the iron staircase to the attic where her apartment occupied three rooms. Once inside she would remove the blindfold. George would take off his clothes and lie on the bed and usually sleep. Adele would leave him there until morning when, upon her return, she too would undress and tell him any news she had before putting on her smock and starting to paint. For the duration of the sitting, usually some days, George was not permitted to leave the apartment, to wear his clothes, to drink alcohol or to smoke.

'Texture, George. It's all down to texture. You square off your canvas. You do what Camus said: you isolate your subject. Sort out your perspective. That's where Leopold went wrong. But after that it's all down to texture. That's where I've been going wrong.'

She was lying naked on the bed. Beside her George was asleep. They were not quite touching, but she could feel the hair on her arms and the back of her neck stand up. He stirred and shifted his left knee towards her when she spoke, but she moved away quickly before contact could be made. A touch would destroy the tension between them, the suspense required for the work. This was another part of the deal, another rule.

It was late. Nearly two. Adele got off the bed and gently draped a blanket over George before putting on some clothes. She had arranged to meet Reid in Harry Lime's at midnight and he would leave soon if she did not arrive. She wrote a note for George and put it on the desk in the other room before leaving the apartment and driving out to the Gürtel and round to the railway station where she parked. Reid was sitting with Peter, his Danish friend, and Januz, George's Yugoslavian assistant, at the management *Stammtisch* at the back of the bar, by the office. Apart from them Harry Lime's was nearly empty. Unusual, but to be expected on a Sunday night at the end of the tourist season. Reid slapped the table in an exaggerated gesture of annoyance when he saw her walking in.

'Shit, Monika, you get worse, I swear.'

'Out of here, Reid, I made it.'

'Yeah, well, you want a beer?'

'Funny man. Melange please, Januz.'

While Januz made her a coffee Reid and Peter resumed their conversation without speaking to her again.

'I don't give a damn about Januz's theories. I just want to know where the shit thing is. Story of the century if I found it.'

'I don't know. I think Januz is maybe right in some ways: if you can work out how this Adele woman's mind works maybe you can find a place to start. As it is we know nothing about her or the painting. Did you try speaking with George again?'

'Yeah, like talking to that wall. I asked him to describe the thing last time. He said it was small and rectangular. Helpful man, you know.'

It had become common knowledge amongst George's regulars at Harry Lime's that his friend, Adele, owned a painting by Egon Schiele. Strangely for Schiele, a painter who was obsessed about his signature, the piece was unsigned. But there was no doubt that the nude study hanging over the desk in the sitting room of her apartment was genuine. She had sufficient documentation which proved that, including a letter from Schiele to the former owner of the work. There was some question, in fact, regarding the ownership of the painting. Leopold Mahler had died intestate and without apparent heir some seventy years before and since that time, until Adele had moved in a year ago, the attic rooms had been kept sealed. Neither Adele nor Leopold's half-sister, Gertrude, had been certain what the legal situation was and nor did they wish to find out, in case the picture was confiscated by the tax office. When Adele had acquired the lease on the studio she had also bought all the furniture and effects. These in themselves were valuable: a table and chairs designed and made by the *Wiener Werkstätte*, antique lamps, an old medicine chest with its contents – including cocaine, morphine and cyanide – intact, an old abacus, shaving equipment and hairbrushes. And there was the painting which was listed on the inventory as 'Picture of naked woman lying on bed'. This complicated the issue further in that Adele was apparently the picture's legal owner. But she doubted the validity of her purchase. Gertrude was well aware that the work was worth millions of schillings but had said that the painting should go to someone who would appreciate it. Why she imagined that Adele, more than any of the other students in her daughter's art class, should appreciate the picture was unclear. But Adele had fallen in love with the Schiele the moment she saw it and had never questioned Gertrude's motives any further.

When Januz returned with Adele's coffee he interrupted Reid and Peter: 'But it was Cesare Pavese who stated that the act of writing poetry is like making love: one may never know if one's own pleasure is shared. This may be true of a certain dimension of writing poetry, or of any creative work, but to my mind it is painting, of all the arts, which comes closest to making love. There are subtleties and details of erotic experience. It is possible, through repetition or near repetition of any given act of lovemaking, to explore those subtleties and details and, for the sensitive lover, this can be rewarding. Similarly I suspect that a sensitive artist could be rewarded by painting the same scene, the same still-life or portrait, using the same light and the same tools, over and over. Ten times, a hundred times, each one rewarding in ways that its predecessor was not. It would be impossible, I believe, to repeat or recreate a work precisely in terms either of form or content. George has told us that his friend, Adele, only ever paints him naked, reclining in the same position on a bed, always under the same conditions. I imagine that each painting is different only in the slightest of respects – a brush stroke here, a shade there – but each one will be noticeably different, despite the fact that the material context is always the same. Adele is not trying to copy something, though – this Schiele of hers, for example. But to recreate something.'

'You do go on, my man . . .'

'Shut up, Reid. Let Januz finish, I'm interested. What I think is amazing is how there was so much suspense in that picture George showed us. He looked as if he was about to jump up and run away. As if he was scared, you know. Did you see that, Monika?'

'I don't know a damn about it.'

'I think you are correct, Peter. Though the fear which Adele painted on George's face was almost certainly not there in reality. I think it exists exclusively in her own mind. Like Schiele, she paints her own emotions quite explicitly onto the face of her subject, reflecting them there. George has not spoken to me of this, but I believe this fear which Adele has is connected with a hope on George's part – a naïve hope in my opinion – that at the end of the sitting she will walk across the room to him and take him, make love to him. What George does not realize is that Adele, like all artists, has her particular fetish. With Adele the fetish is her own virginity. It is what sustains her work. Her fear, then, is not that her subject will leave her, but that he will rape her. Or, if I am exaggerating, that he will at least succeed in seducing her.'

'But really, my man, you do go on. How can you say all that when we've never met the girl and the nearest we've got to her painting is a lousy Polaroid?'

'Since you think yourself an arts critic I had imagined that you might have greater respect for the craft of interpretation, Reid. Knowing you as I do, however . . .'

'I just think there's got to be a better way of finding out who this Adele woman is and more to the point where she lives.'

'And what you going to do when you find it, Reid?'

'Take a fucking photograph, I don't know. Seriously, Monika, I want to find that picture and I want to write it up.'

'Write it up anyway.'

'No evidence. I have been through every piece of paper there is on the subject. I've read every letter Schiele ever wrote or received, I've done everything I can. I just don't see what else I can do except maybe threaten George with a knife.'

'Better make it a machine gun and never turn your back on him again. Hard man, George. Memory like an elephant.'

'You said it, sweetheart. Anyway, I don't think he does know where the place is. Even if he would tell us. Which he won't. Stubborn shit.'

'George is in love with her. He's not going to spill the beans. It would ruin his chances.'

Adele yawned loudly. They were supposed to be going dancing and, though she was not in the mood, she knew she ought to let Reid know that she had not forgotten. In truth it amused her to hear them talk about her and George. Reid was determined to find the painting. The last time she had arranged to meet George, Reid had tried to follow him from the bar in Peter's car, an old Audi. George's new Mercedes was too fast for it and, without even knowing it, he had lost Reid on the Westautobahn. But the fact that Reid had tried to follow George worried her because it showed the lengths to which he was prepared to go to get his story. He had little enough information and since Adele had realized the extent of Reid's interest it had been agreed that George would say nothing further about the picture and only little about Adele and the sittings.

Reid was right. They would never find the painting simply by interpreting the photograph they had seen or analysing what they knew about her relationship with George. Januz's theories interested her, challenged her intellectually and artistically. But they were no threat. Unwittingly he helped her with her work, was on her side, the side of the artist. This she found intriguing: he was a brilliant musician as well as a barman – every night he played blues in Harry Lime's from ten until one. Reid on the other hand was a critic, a *Macher* in Vienna's cultural establishment, albeit a minor one. A minor *Macher* who wanted to be a big-shot. Where Januz had an intuitive understanding of what Adele was doing, Reid was rational in his approach. He had started in the Albertina, in the archives. He had spent weeks there. Then he had visited numerous collectors of Schiele's work in Austria asking if they had any documents, if perhaps they had heard anything about a painting which was thought destroyed by Hitler but which had survived and was hidden by its owner when the Nazis came. He had developed a scenario as a result of his enquiries which was remarkably close to the truth: a friend or patron of Schiele received the painting as a gift, died and the painting, because it was unsigned and unidentified, or perhaps because of some scandal, had been stored and forgotten until Adele found it. His search had been fruitless which was why he was now resorting to cruder methods. She wondered how long it would be before she slipped up. Spilled paint on herself and failed to clean it up properly, or before George said just too much about her. They were careful to cover every angle but simple mistakes could still be made. She had considered involving Reid, taking him into her trust and preventing him from writing his story in that way. But she needed that secrecy in order to paint George as she wished. The process of excluding the outside world from the studio was as important to the work as anything else – the choice of model, the paints, the light.

Reid noticed the yawn and said: 'Hey, Monika. You're two hours late. Let's give U4 a miss. Next time maybe.'

'Sure, Reid. Give me another coffee though.'

'There's got to be a logical way of looking at this. Something I missed. We've tried the painting angle: the way I see it I've got to go for George or Adele or both. What do we know about her?'

'She's pretty.'

'Yeah, but pretty is relative. George is the ugliest shit this side of Mexicoplatz, what's he know about pretty?'

'I'm going to tell him you said that. But you have a point.'

'How many Adeles do you think there are in the phone book?'

'What are you going to do? Call every one of them and say "Hi, are you the Adele with the undiscovered Egon Schiele in your attic studio? My name's Reid and I'd like to blow your whole story." '

'I just say "Is George there?" See what response I get.'

'You're insane.'

'Well, do you have any better suggestions, my friend?'

'Personally I am enjoying the mystery. I have no desire to see it solved.'

'You guys are useless. Anyway, I'm going home. Have to be up early to see a man about an apartment tomorrow. Hey, Monika, you want to meet me? Help me decide on this place.'

When she had left school she studied for two years to be a surveyor, so she was often asked to give friends free advice on whether an apartment was a good deal and how much work would need to be done.

'OK, Reid, if you buy me lunch.'
'Deal. Meet me here at nine.'
'I'll be here by eleven.'
'Fair.'

After Reid had gone Adele and Peter talked for a while and Januz did the books for the week. She liked Peter. He had an innocence similar to that which she saw in George, but with it he was both laconic and sensitive as well. He was a frequent visitor to Vienna – had an apartment in the second district – but since Adele had met him he had been spending much time in Denmark where he had his own business.

'It goes in cycles. Sometimes I have to stay there for six months, sometimes I can work here for six months. One day I'll give up the work there and stay here, I think. Two or three years maybe.'

'I don't know why. This place is boring. I want to leave for a time. Go and live in Spain.'

'Serious?'

'Sure. There's a little village I visited once, near Segovia. Be really great. Except the bullfights. I hate them.'

'Have you been to one?'

'Yeah, lousy. It was one with the guys on horses. Very clever, you know, the way they rode them, but really fucking pointless. Those guys were just on some ego trip. Even though they're all ugly, the women love them because they get in a ring with a stupid bull. I was on the bulls' side.'

'I never went to one, but I have a friend, in Copenhagen, who was a bullfighter. He told me it's all a racket. The managers where he worked, in one city, were very bad. He was a good bullfighter because when they fight, the bulls aren't supposed to suffer too much – I think one of the knives should go into the top of the spine and paralyse them so they don't feel anything, but they still move, and that's the most important bit. He was good at that and he said real Spaniards appreciate it, because that's where the art is. But the people he was working for didn't like it because all the tourists, they want to see some action. So they'd bring in bad bullfighters, guys who missed the spot on the spine and made the bulls go really wild. Lots of blood. Lots of action. Suits the tourists. Quite a few fighters got hurt, so he left and started working at the small fiestas again. He said he didn't want anything to do with the big shows because it was all too corrupt. He's OK, I think.'

'Don't think I'd like him. But yeah, Spain, I'd like to spend a while there. Got a good feel to the place. People talk to each other. Know how to live.'

After another coffee she went back to the studio where George was awake, reading a book. There were no clocks in the apartment and the windows were blacked out so even after one day his sense of time became confused. For Adele this was unimportant. The adrenalin high she experienced during the sittings prevented her from sleeping for more than a couple of hours at a time and she felt fresh as she undressed and gathered together her equipment to continue painting.

Januz was quite right. Recreate was precisely what she was trying to do. The Schiele was covered with a sheet while they worked, to stop it distracting her. Nevertheless, it consumed her thoughts as she worked. Leopold, too, had tried to recreate it, in a different way. She hoped that for her it was an artistic or intellectual exercise. For Leopold it had been a pathological obsession. He had been a pathological person, that much was clear from his diaries. They were beautifully bound in leather, written in immaculate Gothic script, in high German without a trace of Viennese idiom. One hundred pages for every month of his adult life, to the last. Adele had read each volume twice since she moved in, some of them many more times. For the most part they were laughably anguished, adolescent almost in their claims to artistic genius and integrity. But at other times her heart had gone out to him and she empathized with him until she remembered what he had done. Leopold had been born a victim, had lived and died a victim of the circumstances under which he came into the world. But he had killed for his art. For that she could not forgive him.

In 1906 he had attempted to gain entry to the Academy of Fine Arts, the foremost art school in Vienna. It was the same year that Egon Schiele, also sixteen years of age, had succeeded where Leopold failed. That had been the beginning of the obsession which drove Leopold until his death twelve years later. He had not understood from the start how the 'scrawny child' he had met outside the Academy on the day of his examination had persuaded the tutors that he could do what Leopold could not. He had felt usurped, betrayed by his past. The resentment stayed with him but, rather than avoiding Schiele, he sought him out, bought his company, friendship even, with patronage and flattery. The artist had responded readily. And when Schiele did what only the artist can do for his patron, presented him with one of his works, Leopold's inadequacy as a patron, as an artist and as a man finally came to the fore. Convinced, as he had been for twelve years, that he was the equal of Schiele as a painter, of every man in every respect, Leopold attempted to recreate Schiele's masterpiece. The attempt resulted in his own death and in the death of the model he had chosen.

George was asleep again, now. She was sitting outside, on the landing of the iron staircase, wrapped in a blanket and sipping cold coffee, watching the dawn gather. This session had been a good one. Always, after the first full day in the studio, George started to relax, to lose touch with the world outside, to stop worrying about how his business was going or what his friends were doing. His attention focused on Adele, the attic, his own feelings. And she in turn grew more intuitive in her approach to the painting, had to think less about proportions and lines, hues and shades.

He was a beautifully simple man. Harry Lime's was his pride and joy, his masterpiece. He had worked all his life as a barman and had dreamt of owning a place somewhere, not in London but in Europe. A place where there would be no company executives telling him what to sell and at what price, no government insisting that he open at this time and close at that. It was Reid who had suggested the name for the bar. It was a crass suggestion in some ways, but Adele had to concede that it was a good choice, the masterstroke. In the summer George sent people to St Polten to distribute leaflets on the trans-European express trains coming into Vienna, advertising the bar and the fact that it ran an accommodation agency – an exaggeration because all it meant was that hotel touts frequented the place. But the younger tourists came and, finding a warm welcome and other travellers, they came again every night, attracted by the friendly atmosphere and the spirit of occupied Vienna which George contrived to summon up. And in winter, when the tourists were gone, the pimps and their hookers and the black-marketeers would return, drawn by the name of the place, by the atmosphere of seediness which George and Januz set out to create, an atmosphere of illegality, of being beyond the reach of law and order, one which allowed the guests to indulge their fantasies of being on the fringes of society, of being underworld bosses, sharp operators with the city at their feet.

The police put up with it for George was a consummate dealer himself, though his trade was goodwill, tolerance. He was an expansive storyteller, a bon vivant with a magnificently disarming approach. If someone took the slightest offence he would place an arm round their shoulder with a 'You have to be so careful with words. Slippery things and they get slipperier the more you drink. Have an Irish. On the house, my friend.' And in any case, Vienna had not changed so much since the days of the Habsburgs: there was a house commission, voluntary, on any deals that were made. George's clientele celebrated everything they could so they had the excuse to present him with gifts: a crate of cigarettes for Christmas, some electrical goods for his birthday, half a pound of grass because it was Saturday night and the weather had been nice. Some of the gifts inevitably found their way into the homes of bureaucrats and police chiefs who soon came to share George's attitude of live and let live. No one died as a result of a deal made in Harry Lime's. George's world was one of potential: 'Everything is possible, friend. Everything.' He would survey his kingdom with a benevolent smile, breaking up fights if he had to, though never throwing anyone out if they cooled down and settled their differences in a calm and reasonable way. And if someone was ejected they were always welcome to return the next night, or whenever they wished, and start again.

The one thing Adele did not know about Leopold's death was the identity of the model he had killed. She knew some things about her: that, in Leopold's words, she was a young, beautiful, red-haired girl with jewels for eyes. Adele supposed that in real life she must have looked like the girl in Schiele's painting, with sharp features, a sullen expression, thin lips. Leopold was a fool. He had imagined that by finding a model who looked like the girl in the picture he needed only paint exactly what he saw before him. He had failed to understand how much of the work had to come from inside himself. The doctor had said that probably she would have died anyway, of the flu which killed him within days of the murder. But for Adele that was beside the point. He had killed someone who was innocent, who had nothing to do with his obsession. Perhaps that was why she had chosen George as her model, the *Lebenskünstler* as they called him, 'the artist of life'. It was her rejection of Leopold's ethic which held that anything may be done in the name of art: an ethic which Adele considered absurd when she did not find it simply repugnant.

It was light, now, and she decided to sleep for a couple of hours before meeting Reid. She enjoyed pushing herself in that way: working for six, eight hours, sleeping for two and then leaving the apartment and living life as she normally would when she was not painting George. And she enjoyed Reid's company in a perverse way, despite at times being contemptuous of him and the way he saw the world. But he had a point. 'Gotta squirm, baby,' he'd say, 'that way they know you're alive and no shit about it. Accentuate the positive and crash when you can.' It was one way of living your life.

'Monika, you're on time. I don't believe it.'

'Funny man, Reid. Fairly damn funny.'

'OK, it's like this: the place was built in 1840 or so. One of these typical cutesy old-fashioned places, you know. . . .'

'Biedermeier, Reid.'

'Probably, so anyway, it's a good *Hauptmiete*. No strings, full rights. The works.'

'Whose place is it?'

'Some old guy. I mean really old, you know. He's being chucked out by the council. They reckon he's a bit off his head or something. Probably senile. Thing is, he hasn't done any work on the place in years and they'll give me a good grant to fix it up. Structural stuff. Sound OK?'

'Sounds great if the price is right, but it could be pretty high, area like that. They're not meant to, but still . . . Who is this guy?'

'Name's Lasker. Sounds cool, actually. Used to be a waiter in Museum before the war. Before the first war, too. I thought he might have known Schiele. Maybe ask him about it, see if there are any new leads. Anyhow, let's get over there.'

They walked down the Mariahilferstrasse and turned left along a side street where the apartment was on the top floor of a four-storey building in the seventh. When Reid rang the bell a young woman answered and told them she was Nadia, Mr Lasker's home help from the council, until a room was found for him. He was asleep, she said, and she did not want to wake him. But Reid insisted that he had an urgent appointment. Adele always loved the way the Viennese responded to the word 'urgent'. They were let in and Nadia showed them to the dining room and left them to wait. Adele walked around the room looking at the state of the walls and examining floorboards wherever they were visible. The place would need a lot of money over the next couple of years, she told Reid, but it was quite sound from what she could see. She liked it herself. The ceilings were higher than normal and the dining room was huge. Probably every room would be. She opened the French windows and stepped out onto the large south-facing balcony which was in an even greater state of disrepair than the inside. There were terracotta pots lying everywhere, some intact but most of them broken and spilling soil onto the floor. In the middle of the balcony was an old red, metal table with matching chairs around it and a mildewed Coke umbrella slotted through a hole in the centre. Rust was creeping up the table legs and the paint was flaking off.

She went across to the cast-iron railing and leaned over, staring at the ground. When she was a child she used to love going to high-up places with bottles and jars filled with paint which she would drop, just to see the patterns she could make when they broke. She had stopped doing it when she was a teenager and went to the Secession where she saw some bohemian artist throwing pigs' blood and entrails onto a huge clean canvas and, eventually, over sections of the audience. Januz was right when he said all artists have their fetishes. She was pleased that her fetish, as Januz had described it, was relatively innocuous. Reid joined her a moment later and they sat down at the table.

'So, what do you say?'

'It's great. Couldn't put a price on it exactly, of course. How much can you afford?'

'Up to a hundred.'

'You're talking about fifty just to put some new plaster on the walls and sort out some of those boards. Probably needs rewiring, too.'

'Thought maybe I'd take the plaster off. Have bare brick. Perhaps paint that, probably not. The council should cover some of it, anyway.'

'Yeah, would be cheaper in the short run I guess. You should find out when they last had a new roof. What's the ground rent?'

'Thousand a month. Not bad at all.'

'I love this balcony. Be great in the summer.'

'I know. And see: we're not overlooked at all.'

At that moment the sitting room doors swung open and Lasker hobbled out onto the balcony. Adele was amazed by his face, like an old monkey's, all shrivelled up and crinkled into a confused frown. He squinted at them and said: 'Greetings, greetings. Are you Reid? And your friend. . . .'

'Monika.'

'Welcome, welcome, let us return inside where it is warmer and we can drink some tea before Nadia shows you the apartment. Or would you prefer to look around first, Reid, while the tea is being prepared?'

'Perhaps that would be best, Mr Lasker. Then we can discuss things.'

'Very well, very well.'

Nadia showed them around, watching them carefully as if they might steal something. Then they went back into the large sitting room and sat down on the sofa opposite Lasker. They sat in silence for a few moments as Lasker packed a pipe. While they waited Adele looked around the sitting room. It was like a junkyard, filled with broken ornaments, ancient and unidentifiable machines with springs and gears erupting from their insides, battered books, photographs and postcards from around the world. Over the fireplace hung a framed photograph of the inside of Café Museum as it had been a long time before, and on the mantelpiece another photograph in a frame, but the image so faded as to be almost invisible against the yellowing paper on which it had been printed. Only the faintest outline of three figures could be seen, a man and his two children, she thought.

'Well?'

'How much?'

'Let us have some tea first. After a fashion with which I imagine you are unfamiliar.'

Nadia handed each of them a small cup of dark, strong looking tea and Lasker intoned:

'The first cup has no sugar in it because life, at times, can be very bitter.'

They drained the cups in one swallow and Nadia took them and handed out a second cup each.

'The second cup contains much sugar because life at times is very sweet.'

Adele nearly retched because she hated sweet things anyway and the cup contained more sugar than tea.

'The final cup contains just the correct amount of sugar. . . . Need I say more? I thought not. You are intelligent people. Unusually so for young people today.'

She liked him, she decided. He wasn't senile and anyway, she liked people who talked about the nature of life with complete strangers. He smiled back at her and said, in a loud but conspiratorial aside: 'Are you lovers?'

Adele opened her mouth to reply but Lasker laughed and said:'I am only teasing. When you reach my age you too will seek humour wherever you can find it. There is little enough to laugh about in the world. So, Reid. You like it.'

'Yes, if the price is fair.'

'Fifty thousand and cheap at the price. No discussions, take it or leave it. I could get more. Fifty thousand and it's yours.'

'OK. Deal.'

Reid reached over and offered his hand to Lasker who glanced at it and, after a moment, said: 'My word not good enough for you? Very well.'

Before Reid could answer Adele asked: 'Mr Lasker, Reid told me you worked in Museum. Is that right?'

'Indeed. For many years.'

He waved his hand in the direction of the photograph over the fireplace. 'It was better then, of course.'

'Did you know Schiele? Egon Schiele?'

'Schiele? Of course. Schiele, Klimt, many others. I served them all. Though you should understand, Reid, that I was a waiter. It was not my place to know these people intimately.'

'But could you tell me anything about the people Schiele knew?'

'Very little, Reid. There were so many of them: many would-be artists, people who wished to be seen with him and the others. With Klimt I had more contact, through a friend. This--' he jabbed a bony finger at the faded photograph on the mantelpiece —'this photograph was coloured in by Gustav Klimt himself. The colour has long since bled from it, of course, but still. . . .'

'Tell us about it.'

Reid glared at her, annoyed that she was asking about something he considered irrelevant. But she shrugged, refusing to be intimidated.

'Tell you about it? It is a long story. I shall ask Nadia to bring us coffee before I start. If you are sure you wish to hear it.'

'Yes, we do. How long did you work in Museum?'

'Nearly thirty years. From 1909 until Hitler came. Then I went with my family to America for the duration of the war and the occupation. I returned on the very day the State Treaty was signed. Nadia, we should now like some coffee.'

The social worker frowned but she went away and duly returned a few minutes later with a cup of coffee for each of them.

'She kept trying to bring me decaffeinated coffee at first. And hid my pipe. These people have no imagination. They fail to realize how they would feel in my position and no amount of reasoning seems to help them. I showed her how difficult old people can be, however. I went on hunger strike until she agreed to give me real coffee and let me smoke my pipe in peace. You can imagine the scandal were I to die of starvation whilst under her care.'

Adele wanted to ask why he was being moved into a home, but she was unsure whether it would be rude: for all she knew he was simply incontinent. He packed his pipe again, lit it and began his story.

'Things in those days were relatively good for our people. Lueger, the Mayor of Vienna at the time, said that he hated Jews, but in truth this was rhetoric which he ignored once it had served its purpose of winning him votes. He had many Jewish friends, some of whom I knew. However, it was still difficult to get certain jobs unless you had the contacts, you see. All my life I had wanted to become a waiter in a coffee house. I would go often to Museum or to Central and sit for hours watching them at work as they served the customers. They had an unusual dignity, one to which I aspired.

'I was fortunate. My sister, Emma, had made the acquaintance of a wealthy and aristocratic man who was great friends with Klimt and, I dare say, associated with the others of the Secession group. His name was Karl and he was an artist himself, though very much the gentleman amateur. He spent a great deal of his time in Museum and when Emma, with whom he was quite in love, mentioned my ambition to him, it was as good as a command. Doubtless it helped that my father, in fact, was not Jewish, but whatever: he arranged it and I started within the month. Further-more, as we were close enough in age – he was only two years older than I – we became firm friends.

'My parents would not allow Emma to marry Karl. Not because of his religion, of course not. But because he already had, by a previous relationship, the most beautiful twin daughters I have ever had the pleasure to lay my eyes upon. They were illegitimate, though to be fair it must be said that had their mother survived childbirth I am quite certain that Karl would have married her. He was a rascal, but he was a man of honour who hated hypocrisy more than anything except Germans. Karl worshipped Maria and Clara above anything else in his life. No matter how busy he was with his friends or his mistresses or his businesses, he always found time to spoil them and give them the best. Until the war started, that is.

'I was fortunate. I knew many people who were in a position to help me avoid conscription. Karl himself helped me. I had no loyalty to Franz Joseph; Franz Ferdinand was a good man but his death was no reason to start a war. And indeed, I was something of a socialist in those days, as were many Jews of my generation. I had met Trotsky once, I read his newspaper. Why would I have wished to fight for one imperial power against another? Karl, however, was obliged to serve, and wished to. He never actually fought because he was a strategist, one of the few good ones the Empire had. It resulted in his being absent from Vienna for the duration of the war. He never managed to return, not once.

'I occasionally saw Maria and Clara over the next years. As you should know, those of us who remained in Vienna continued to lead a very civilized existence, as if there were no war. Only the lack of certain consumer items and a shortage of young men were noticeable. As they grew older Maria and Clara spent more and more time in Museum meeting with the artists who still came there. Maria seemed to be following in her father's footsteps because she was becoming a talented artist herself. And as they became young women, they grew even more beautiful.

'Karl had asked me to keep an eye on them and see that they were well and needed for nothing. It did occur to me at times that their guardian allowed them greater freedom than might have been expected, but it was wartime and besides, what could I have done? For all my friendship with their father, I was just a waiter in a coffee house and a Jew to boot. I had no right to instruct them how to behave. When I saw them I asked after their health, if they had any troubles, but they were always in high spirits and the men they were with seemed to be of respectable character, or as respectable as artists can be. I continued with my life, married a beautiful woman, had children of my own. All I wanted was to survive the war, wait for things to change – as they were bound to – and to continue with my comfortable existence as a waiter in a Viennese coffee house. Karl wrote me occasionally, though never more than a few lines of greeting and news of the war; he never suggested that there were problems with the girls. By the time he returned to Vienna, at the very end of 1918, the girls' guardian was dead of the flu that killed so many people that year. Clara had married some ridiculous Prussian diplomat and Maria, Maria was gone.

'There was nothing Karl hated more than Prussians. He was a proud Viennese – you should have heard the language he used in 1933 when Hitler became Chancellor. Had he been alive in 1938 I am quite sure he would have fought the Germans with his bare hands. But Clara was as strong willed as he and his mother before him. She refused to leave her husband as Karl demanded – she could have done so easily because she was a Catholic whereas he was a Protestant – and in defiance of Karl's wishes they moved together to Berlin and only returned to Austria when he was dead and Schuschnigg was Chancellor of the Republic. I never saw her after her marriage except once, in 1936, and if she recognized me she gave no sign of it.

'Maria was the mystery. No one, but no one, knew where she was, if she was alive or dead, in Vienna or on the moon. Karl searched for her everywhere. He visited me every day in Museum asking if I had any news of her, could give him any clue as to where she might be. And, in truth, there were things I could have told him. They were not pleasant and I was reluctant because I did not see how they could help. Better, I thought, for Karl not to know. Maria, you see, became a courtesan. Not, I heard, for the money, but for the fun. It was impossible for me to tell Karl this, that his daughter was little better than a common whore. It would have upset him too much and I thought it would be best for him to remember her as the innocent fourteen-year-old she was when he last saw her. Perhaps I was wrong, but that was the decision I made.

'It was in November of 1918 that I saw her for the last time – in the week that Schiele died, if that interests you – and, indeed, I suspect that I was amongst the last to see her alive. The man was a little wild, with a long black coat such as our people used to wear, though he was no Jew, and wearing a hat. When I saw them it was late at night and not in Museum, but on the Ringstrasse, near the Schwarzenbergplatz. They both seemed drunk and he was pushing her around, perhaps playfully, perhaps not. Now, I cannot be certain that it was Maria, but she had the same red hair, whoever she was, and a certain posture, an . . . abandon would be the word. Naturally I considered challenging the man but by then I had heard enough of Maria's adventures to feel that she had outgrown any care I might have been able to give, for all her youth. I do not know to this day, but I suspect that I should have done something. He was one of those bohemian types who look as though they have stepped from the gutter but who, in all probability, are wealthy enough. I remember him staring at me, a wild stare. It unnerved me. I have lived with that and it is enough. I would not wish to have lived with the added burden of a close friend's misery on my account. I suspect that the man recognized me from Museum, but in any event I saw neither him nor Maria again.

'It is difficult to make out the features, now, but the figure on the right is Maria – she was slightly taller than Clara at that age, I remember. The photograph was taken by myself on the day before Karl went away to the war. It was a glorious day and Karl and I took the girls into the Vienna woods for a picnic. He had bought the camera only that week and he asked me if I would take a picture of the three of them. I did not see my handiwork until after the war, however. When Karl returned. By then, as a favour to Karl, Klimt had coloured it. I must say that the likeness was a striking one – not my doing, of course, as I had never held a camera in my life and never have since. Over the next years Karl kept the picture in his study where the sun could shine on it, making the colours truly glow. One could imagine that it was not a photograph, but a window, looking onto the past, onto another, perhaps better time. I told him that the colours would fade, but as he often said: better to enjoy the picture than to stick it away in the dark, and I dare say he was right.

'The last time I saw Karl was in 1934. He had not spoken of

the girls in years, though the fact that he never married suggested perhaps that they were always on his mind. We had dinner together and afterwards coffee in his study. We spoke mostly of recent news, that the Nazis had killed their own people. He urged me to leave Austria, to go to America, because he knew that more trouble was stirring here, too. As much as anything, he knew of my involvement with the Socialists in February of that year and, I suspect, had protected me in some way. Before I left he took the photograph down and we looked at it for a long time. Klimt's colours had faded into nothingness. "Franz," he said, "they have gone now. The girls have gone." And he handed it to me and told me to keep it: I had taken the photograph and now that the colours were gone it should be mine again. That night he killed himself. The newspapers said it was because he had been discovered plotting against Dolfuss, but I have never believed that. His heart was broken. There was nothing else to it. There were also some letters he gave me. Including one from Klimt. Perhaps you would like to see it? It is here somewhere . . .'

While Lasker packed his pipe again and started to rummage through a pile of papers on the floor Adele went onto the balcony again. She was sure that Maria was the woman Leopold had killed. The date – the week Schiele had died – was certainly correct; Maria was red-haired; the description of Leopold, wearing the coat and hat which still hung behind the door of the studio, fitted. Somehow it made it worse to know something about the girl's life, to know the name of her father, her sister, to have spoken to someone who himself had known her, to have seen a photograph, albeit faded, of her as a child. She decided that she would return and visit Lasker without Reid and tell him how Maria's life had ended, if he wished to know. And there were other things he could tell her, she was sure.

Adele paled when she read the letter from Klimt. There were only three sentences of relevance, but Adele knew that they would be enough for Reid: 'I spoke to S. the other day – he says he will exhibit at the Prater provided that G. is permitted to exhibit as well. I've told him that he is a fool – G. is no painter – but S. says that he owes him the favour and furthermore that he feels sorry for him (you know, of course, about the terrible accident with G.'s father and that bitch of an Italian of his – at their factory – it was in the news last month). He also says he will give him a piece which is nearly worse, because however much he is worth, G. is a philistine.'

Reid read the letter over and over, apparently unable to grasp what was written.

'G. This must be him, Monika. It has to be.'

'So how do you work that out?'

'OK, it's a long shot. But as far as I know I never came across anyone with an initial G. who might have been given a painting. The Prater exhibition – that was an exhibition of war art. I always thought it was strange for Schiele to be there at all, but if there was some guy who did him a favour. . . .'

'If this S. is Schiele.'

'May I ask what it is you wish to discover?'

'Sorry, Mr Lasker. Do you know who this G. person is?'

'I am afraid not. Klimt had so many associates. Schiele as well. There can be little doubt that S. is Schiele, however. If you will excuse me, Monika, Reid, I am tired now. It has been a pleasure to share some time and this story with you both, but I fear I must sleep.'

'Thank you Mr Lasker. I'll arrange a lawyer and I'll come by again soon.'

'As you wish. Come in a few days and I will have the agreement ready. It is a simple one with few conditions.'

Outside Reid was excited.

'Right. I'm going straight to the Albertina to find out the names of everyone who exhibited at that thing in the Prater. You want to come?'

'No thanks, Reid. I've had enough for one day. Say we meet later . . . in Jocherl? Sixish?'

'Sounds good. I think Januz is free this evening, I'll get him and Peter along too. See you then.'

Adele felt numb as she walked back to Harry Lime's to pick up her car. Reid would still have problems tracing her address on the basis of Leopold's surname because he had been another bastard, the son of a peasant girl from near Hollabrun. It was ironic: Leopold's mother, too, had died giving birth and her father had brought the baby to Vienna and presented it to Hans Mahler who gave him some money and agreed to take the child. At that point Hans was unmarried. His own father ran the family business and was content for Hans to enjoy his youth before he in turn started working for the company. The child was welcomed into the household and Hans, it seemed, enjoyed the notoriety he gained by having a bastard son at the age of only seventeen. Many young women seized upon the opportunity of visiting baby Leopold as a means to seeing and attempting to win the favour of the eldest son of such a powerful industrial family. When Leopold was four he gained a stepmother, a beautiful Italian aristocrat named Alessandra, who insisted that Leopold be disinherited as soon as she herself bore children. She had three daughters but no sons, which was a disappointment to Hans. As Leopold and the girls grew older, Alessandra's demands grew stricter: Leopold was forbidden to use the name Mahler; he was to live in the attics so that he could not interfere with the girls' games; he was to have no property of his own; he was never to eat with the family . . .

For all that, Hans was a fair father who looked after his son as best he could. He gave him a substantial allowance drawn against a secret trust of which Alessandra had no knowledge, he took him out with his friends and spent what time he could with him, allowed him as much freedom as he wished by way of compensation for the security he could not have. Leopold was a poor little rich kid who had everything but who had nothing, not even a name. But Reid was not stupid: he would surely find out who G. was, who Leopold was, and there was nothing Adele could think of to stop him.

She was not sure how long she had. It might take Reid a day or it might take a month or anything in between to fill in the details. There were, of course, possibilities. She could try to remove everything from the attic before Reid got there. But that was not the point: Reid needed only to go to the police and he would soon discover that Adele was the Monika he knew. Another option, of course, was to confess to him, as she had thought of doing before, in the hope that his respect for their friendship would prevent him from publishing the story. But she was under no illusions: Reid would certainly resent the fact that she had kept the painting hidden from him. In any case, she simply did not want Reid or anyone to know that she was Adele. She decided to return to the studio and speak to George. If anyone could suggest a solution, she thought, George was the one.

Adele was in Jocherl, in the eighth, by five. She had argued with George about what to do: when she had explained everything he suggested that he speak with Reid and, if necessary, threaten him, force him to give up what he was doing. Adele said that was stupid, because he would realize that she had told George about the visit to Lasker's and anyway he would carry on with his search but would keep it secret from the rest of them. To resort to violence was against her principles, she said. George replied that in that case he did not care if Reid did find out where the painting was. He was not ashamed to model for Adele, what did it matter? If they moved the painting to one of his friends' apartments there would be no proof that they had ever had it, Reid would be no better off than he was before. They ended up shouting at each other, then sat in silence for over an hour.

And the worst of it was that she had not progressed with the painting all day. Only George's sketched outline and part of his torso was on the canvas, a shapeless layer of gouache. Her concern about Reid and when he would arrive made her nervous. She could not paint when she expected him to walk through the door at any moment. She had tried, she had removed her clothes and put on her smock, but it was no good and she had to leave. She made George promise to stay there until she returned. 'A deal's a deal, isn't it?' he'd said. First she had gone to Museum where she sat alone for a while drinking a coffee, then she walked through the underground passage below Karlsplatz to the Wienzeile and went into the Secession where she spent half an hour studying the Beethoven frieze in the basement. After that she had walked for a while longer, not going anywhere in particular but allowing the roads to lead her. She had ended up at Harry Lime's where she sat with Januz for a while, not talking much, before taking a tram back to the centre, picking up her car and driving to Jocherl.

Januz, Peter and Reid arrived at the coffee house together at just after six.

'Monika, you OK? This is twice you've been on time today. What's with you?'

'Get lost, Reid. I came to read the paper. Been here an hour already.'

'Guess who's a clever bastard.'

'What did you find out?'

'A name, that's all. Tell you later when we've had some beers to celebrate.'

When Januz ordered his drink the waiter, who had just come on duty, pretended not to understand his German. Adele snapped at him, telling him that he had some kind of a problem and did he know there were laws in Austria against racism. It was a problem which Januz often had in coffee houses where his dark skin made him stand out amongst the other customers. It was true that there were bars in some districts where a Yugoslav or a Turk would be refused entry. But coffee houses were supposed to be above that and the waiter became icily polite when he realized that Adele herself was Viennese.

When the drinks had arrived Januz told them about the book he was reading.

'Apparently Bokassa beat up some suspected criminals and three of them died. Waldheim, who was Secretary General of the United Nations at the time, complained about this or something and Bokassa went crazy and called him "a pimp, a colonialist and an imperialist". I wonder, perhaps, if Bokassa knew things which the rest of us did not at the time.'

'Probably they used to have breakfast together.'

'Don't, please, Reid. You know, two nights ago I was walking past the Hofburg and there was a big crowd hanging around outside, so I decided to go in and have a look. I just pretended I belonged there so the cops didn't stop me. A film company had taken the place over to shoot some movie about the war. It was incredible. The courtyard was decked out with swastikas and cardboard tanks and everyone was in army gear and stuff. Right outside Waldheim's office. I can't believe that he would allow such a thing.'

'It's because he wants everyone to think he's liberal and has a clean conscience. Typical Austrian reasoning, Peter.'

'Clean conscience. You're joking, Monika.'

At that Peter stood up and did a Nazi salute and shouted across the café: 'The man is a pimp, furthermore an imperialist and, in addition, a colonialist.'

The waiter came running over and almost pushed him back into his seat saying that this was a Viennese coffee house, not a Bavarian beer cellar. When he had gone away again Peter said: 'I want that man for lunch tomorrow, but stew him well.'

'I wouldn't joke about it, my man. Look in that guy's eyes; he'd have you for a snack as soon as look at you. You know how these Austrians like their meat. So, Monika, you want to hear what I found out?'

Monika shrugged. 'Why not.'

'Gauckerl. Leopold Gauckerl. He's the only name with a "G" of all the people who exhibited at that exhibition who I think's a contender.'

'So that's all you got? Bet he's not in the phone book.'

'Come on, Monika. It's a start. Anyway, by the time I tracked down a catalogue of the exhibition it was too late to go to the records office. No rush. I'll go tomorrow. I should have his address by the evening. You want to come and help?'

'Reid, have you considered what the implications of this might be?'

'What implications are they, Januz?'

'In all probability George will break your arms at least. . . .'

'No, no, no, he'll have his balls.'

'Or as Peter rightly says, he may have your balls. That is a start. But also what about this Adele woman? The painting is her personal property; she is under no obligation to allow you into her apartment; more to the point she clearly does not wish for others to know of the painting's existence or who she is or, indeed, anything about this matter. It is questionable whether you have the right to go into this. At least one can say that you are entitled to find out the whereabouts of the painting, but you should consider well if it is right to publicize that information or to challenge Adele. You could do much harm.'

'Since when did you give a damn about all that ethics shit, Januz? You said yourself it's a question of public interest if there is a Schiele which hasn't been seen before.'

'And I am not certain now that it is. There is also the detail that this discovery would be good for your career.'

'That's OK for you to say, Mr Bar Manager, but what about me? Anyway, look: I've got as much respect as the next person for individual privacy and all that stuff. But we're talking about something which people should be allowed to hear about. If you have to know, I think there may well be some legal questions in there: I'd bet good money that the tax people would be very keen to hear about all this. So, I don't like tax people any more than the rest of us. I change names, keep the location a secret, get a good photo of the thing and leave our Adele friend in peace. Won't hurt a soul.'

'I hope your conscience remains clean afterwards. I hope your conscience has no reason to feel bad, I should say.'

Reid did not answer but Adele could not tell if it was because he was thinking about what Januz had said or if he was simply annoyed that the issue had been raised.

Januz ordered another drink for everyone, coffee for Adele. He was loyal to George in a way that Reid could not possibly understand. He saw in his boss the same innocence that she saw, the same childlike seriousness which helped him run his bar so well. It was an innocence which, Adele thought, Januz had lost a long time before, if he had ever had it. But he was aware of its existence in others and, perhaps conscious of his own worldly cynicism, he appreciated it and sought to protect it. There were, Adele knew, many things which happened at Harry Lime's of which George would not approve and from which Januz shielded him. The trade in false passports, for example, would have appalled George whose view was that people's misery should not be exploited in the way that the misery of the guest workers often was. Januz was more pragmatic: he knew that the demand for passports had to be satisfied and that even if the forgers and the bureaucrats were making vast sums from the business, it was what the guest workers wanted and often needed in order to stay in Vienna. Adele did not suppose that there was anything Januz could do in this case. She doubted whether Reid would listen to him or any pleas he might make on George's behalf. He would absorb Januz's arguments and arrange his own around them, justifying them out of existence. And Januz did not realize that the fact of Reid's knowing Adele's identity was the crucial element, that in destroying the exclusivity of her work, it would ruin the project.

It had been the same for Leopold. He had barely left the apartment in the ten months after he received the painting from Schiele. In that time there had been a constant stream of models entering and leaving the building, prostitutes many of them, who had answered his advertisements in the press. Some of them he attempted to paint, most of them he sent away with a few crowns as soon as he saw them, telling them they were unsuitable. Only Maria did he specifically seek out. He had seen her before, in Museum, and must have known long before he went to see her that she was the model he wanted, though there was no mention of her in his diaries until the last three days. When he did find her his entry in the diary was rhapsodic and kitsch, but so contrived that Adele had the feeling he had rehearsed it a hundred times before writing it. When he found her he spent those three days trying to paint her as he thought Schiele would have. After that sentimentalist outpouring about Maria, the entries were sparse and terse until the final entry which read: 'Schiele dead. Flu. Must go on.' She had not been sure whether he meant that Schiele had died of flu or if he knew that he himself was coming down with the symptoms and did not have long to live.

Adele had tried to imagine Leopold's frustration with the girl, the anger building up in him as his model, who must have been feverish, failed to pose in 'the right way', anger which he typically directed at Maria instead of at his own incompetence. He had strangled her with his bare hands. And even after she was dead he had attempted to move her limbs into the right position and paint her. So the doctor had said after examining her broken bones. And, ironically, it was probable that Maria had given Leopold the flu which killed him. A justice of sorts. It was several days later when they opened the attic and Gertrude had told her the stench was awful. Sometimes, at night, when she was alone, Adele had imagined she could smell it leaking from the floorboards or the walls and she would have to leave the studio, go somewhere, anywhere to escape it.

She excused herself to the others, saying she felt tired. After arranging to meet Reid in Museum the following day she went back to her apartment. She would work all night, the imminence of Reid's arrival a spur to her: she had to finish this painting before he discovered her whereabouts.

She reached Museum at one, half an hour later than she had arranged but she was still there before Reid. She had kept George awake all night with coffee and had continued working until she had to leave. The painting was almost complete, only the detail on the face needed to be finished. She was pleased with it. She had captured the outlines perfectly, and the texture too was right. This evening she would finish it, after she had stalled Reid for a while. He arrived, out of breath and laughing.

'I'm getting worse than you, Monika. Sorry: I just filled in the rest of the details.'

'All of them?'

'Nearly. I haven't found out who lives there now – I'll do that this afternoon – but I know where Leopold Gauckerl's place is. Gauckerl. What a name. If you want to know, it was the name of Mozart's pet dog, so someone had a sense of humour. Anyway, I checked up on him and there was no Leopold Gauckerl to be found. Bad news. But then I thought I'd see if there was something I could do with what Klimt hinted about G.'s father. Look: it's from the paper.'

Reid pulled a photocopy from his pocket and handed it to her. 'See? "Hans Mahler and his wife Alessandra were killed in the explosion at their armaments factory yesterday. The factory was recently converted to the production of" blah blah blah . . . The way I see it Leopold was illegitimate and his parents didn't want him using their name on his paintings. Especially if they were as bad as all that. Well, I checked it out – it was easy in the end – and the Mahlers lived at 15 —gasse. In the third fucking district, can you believe. Leopold Mahler, when I finally got there, died of flu in November 1918. No address listed, but I reckon that would be him. Only one way to find out, though.'

'You want to go now?'

'No, no. Januz and Peter want to come along too and Januz

isn't free until nine. A bit late, I think. Probably they just want to make sure I behave myself when I get there. You want to come too?'

'Maybe. Hey, Reid: shall we do something for the afternoon?'

'Such as? I did want to try and check out who lives in this place now. No good if Adele turned out to be Waldheim's best mate's bit on the side, would it?'

'Not very likely.'

'You don't know George.'

'Maybe a gallery.'

'You hate galleries, Monika.'

'Yeah, but sometimes, you know. More modern stuff. Or in the Belvedere – get you in the mood for discovering this Schiele.'

'OK, if you're sure. You driving?'

When they arrived they paid and went straight to the first floor, to the rooms where the Jugendstil collection was on display. Adele led Reid to a painting by Klimt – *Judith and Holofernes*.

'Look.'

'Yeah, not Schiele.'

'But look.'

'Do you know the story?'

'Holofernes was Nebuchadnezzar's general, besieging some city.'

'And Judith agreed to sleep with him, but then she killed him and saved her city.'

'Klimt was afraid of women.'

'Woman goes around doing that, who wouldn't be?'

'I had a dream about you last night, Reid.'

'Nothing decent, I hope.'

'I was lying in bed. I was cradling your head in my arms.'

'So what was I doing?'

'Nothing, Reid. It was just your head. You were dead, I think.'

'Great, Monika. Just great.'

'I was her. Judith.'

'And I was Holofernes?'

Adele laughed at Reid, his voice sounding so meek.

'No, Reid. You just had his eyes.'

Reid shook his head and passed on to a sculpture which was on loan to the museum, a Rodin. Adele stayed with the Klimt for a while. She loved the way he turned his frames into integral parts of his paintings, something assertive and proud of their function. Or something which invaded the paintings themselves. After a while she joined Reid who had gone through to the next room and was sitting cross-legged on the floor staring at a late Schiele, desire written on his face.

'There's a world in that painting.'

'There's a world outside it. C'mon.'

She pulled him to his feet and they wandered around for a while until she slipped her arm through his and led him back down the stairs and outside where they sat looking down the gardens towards the city centre.

'Say we go for a coffee.'

'Shit, Monika, coffee. It's always coffee with you.'

'OK, a drink then.'

'You, drink?'

'Sure, it's been known. There's a bar not far from here. It's great, really dirty. You'll hate it.'

'And see you drink? You're on.'

The bar she knew was near her place, in the third, close to the old slaughterhouse. Inside it was smoke-filled and busy with workers who had been on the early shift at the factories nearby. The other customers turned to look when they came in and the bar became quieter. She noticed Reid's horror as he took in the red plastic seats, the vinyl tablecloths, the plastic flowers which were practically black with grease and smoke. There was a table free by the window so they sat down and the old woman behind the bar came over to take their order – a beer each.

'Monika, what in Christ's name is this place?'

'Neat, don't you think? Don't worry about it, Reid. No one's going to knife you – I know all these people.'

He looked uncomfortable in his smart jacket and shirt but gradually he relaxed as the other customers lost interest and went back to their conversations.

'This is my sort of place, Reid. These guys are fun, you know. Bet you didn't know I go to football matches with some of them every Saturday and truck racing whenever it's on. Good bunch of guys. Nothing to be scared of.'

'I'm not scared, I'm just surprised. Never thought this would be your kind of scene.'

'And we all go skiing together in the winter, things like that. Actually, skiing isn't quite right. But we go away and have a good time. Most of them can't ski.'

The old woman behind the bar was watching her intently and Adele nodded to her, upon which she broke into a toothless grin and came over and tapped Reid on the shoulder. He started and looked round, leaning away from the woman as she pushed her face close up to his and greeted him in a variation of Viennese dialect that even Adele found difficult to follow. Then she went back to the bar and returned a moment later with three schnapps glasses and a bottle. She poured one for each of them. Adele said: 'She likes you, Reid. You're getting the star treatment. But don't breathe in when you drink this. Down it in one and chase it with a good shot of beer, OK? You die otherwise.'

Reid nodded, bewildered, and they toasted each other cheerfully – Reid uncertainly – before downing their drinks. Reid did as Adele had told him and managed to say, 'Wasn't so bad,' before he belched, tasted the schnapps at the back of his throat and vomited onto the table. Adele and the old woman stifled their laughter as Reid collapsed sideways, groaning with embarrassment as much as nausea. The old woman went to get a cloth and they cleaned the table while Reid went to the toilets to wash his face, the other customers still laughing at the entertainment.

When he returned Adele said, 'Cross between diesel oil and raw potato? Probably what it is, but face it, Reid, you'll never be accepted in Austria until you can take home-made schnapps like a man.'

She knew he would rise to the bait and, sure enough, after demanding another beer, he filled their glasses again. An hour later he was unconscious and two of the workers who had been watching the spectacle carried him out to Adele's car and laid him gently on the back seats, shaking their heads uncomprehendingly.

Reid was still unconscious when she parked the car outside the monastery on the Leopoldsberg. Adele left him there while she walked round the outer wall to the viewing platform on the other side of the hill from where people could look out over the Danube and the east side of the city. The hill was named after the ruler of Austria who ransomed Richard I of England. With the ransom he decided to build a new town wherever the handkerchief he dropped from the top of the Leopoldsberg landed. So she had been told, though history was never her strong point. Adele often came here with George to look over the city and towards the town, Kloster-neuburg. It put Harry Lime's into perspective for George, the Schiele for her. After a few minutes she returned to the car.

Reid had started to snore so he did not, at least, have alcohol poisoning. He had drunk most of the bottle himself, not even noticing that she had stopped after her third glass and slipped out to the toilet where she forced herself to throw up. She dragged him by the feet from the car and then hooked her hands under his armpits and pulled him over to the low wall at the side of the car park, where the hillside dropped steeply down into the woods. She propped him up against it and sat down beside him. His head lolled over and rested on her shoulder but after moving him twice she let him be.

'Texture, Reid. It's all about texture. Texture and perspective. People like you, Reid . . . You see the world so simply, don't you. In black and white and two dimensions, because you don't know how to see it any other way. Just like Leopold Gauckerl. He tried to copy the Schiele, Reid. But he didn't know what he was doing. He didn't realize that Schiele painted that thing standing on top of a step-ladder, six feet off the ground, looking down at his model. There was no way anyone could have got into the position Leopold thought he saw in that painting. But he tried. Just like you would have tried. You're just like him, Reid. You fit the world around you, make it the way you want it to be.'

Suddenly she slapped him on the face, a hard slap which echoed against the monastery walls. He barely stirred, just dribbled a little from the corner of his mouth and fell sideways as she stood up. She kicked him viciously, but more self-consciously, in the thigh, walked over to her car and drove away from the monastery without looking back.

By the time she reached the nineteenth she was calmer, but still shocked by the depth of her anger. Reid was on the verge of destroying her life, ruining her work: she had wanted, just for an instant, to see him dead, to strangle him, to throw him over the hillside. The violence with which she had slapped him had diverted her from that, but she knew that the impulse had been there. Maybe, she was not sure, maybe she understood Leopold's anger now. A rage caused by lack of vision and little else – she had only herself to blame. She headed for Harry Lime's, driving fast and cutting up anyone who got in her way. She had to see Januz, just to get things into perspective, to start herself thinking sensibly again. She was not sure what she would do, if she would tell him the truth, but the Yugoslav's view on things was always so clear that even if she disagreed with what he said she came away from any conversations they had with a clear view of her own.

'No sign of George?'

Januz looked up from the book he was reading when Adele walked into the office, apparently pleased to see her.

'No. He is normally several days. But I wish I could contact him, to let him know.'

'Reid didn't give you the address, then?'

'No. You?'

She shook her head as she took off her jacket and sat down.

'I do not like what our friend is doing, Monika. His career is successful enough without this, whatever he says. It will be of service to no one. And George, George will be very angry. That is what I worry about most of all.'

'Never seen George angry.'

'I have, once. It was last year and we were together at a concert in the Stadthalle. Some Austrians started shouting at me, the usual things. It had been a bad day. We had been to the funeral of a friend of George's in the morning and in the afternoon he had to sack a barman for stealing drinks. He started hitting these Austrians: before I knew what was happening four of them were unconscious, one with a broken arm. The other two ran away. I will go with Reid tonight. But only for his own safety. He does not realize.'

'Maybe Reid deserves to get kicked.'

'Possibly so, but he does not deserve to die. Where is he now?'

'He went off somewhere. Something about the records office.'

'It is a great shame. Reid is like a young child who is compelled to break things open in order to see how they work. Even when he has no right to do so. He is never content with the mystery of things even when it is clear that to examine closer will bring no advantage whilst destroying the mystery as well. He tries to do the same thing with people. Not with us, but with others.'

'Like with Adele.'

'Possibly, though Adele interests him less than the simple physical existence of this Schiele. "How can this be?" he asks himself. He is unimaginative in this way. He needs the concrete, whatever he thinks about it.'

'So what do you think George will do?'

'I truly do not know. But I think he will hurt Reid. Someone, anyway, will be hurt tonight.'

They spoke for a short while longer and then Adele said that she had to go.

'Will you come tonight?'

'Perhaps. If I do I'll see you here.'

'At nine or so.'

When she reached her block she double-parked outside and remained sitting in the car for some minutes, her hands clenching the steering wheel tightly. She felt exhausted, mentally and physically, now. But she had to gather together what energy remained. She had to finish the painting before Reid, Januz and Peter arrived. And then what? Januz had told her things she had been unaware of. About George and the extent of his commitment to what they were doing, his commitment to her. George had confided some of his feelings to Januz, feelings which he could not express directly to her but which, perhaps, she had caught in her studies of him. 'Adele is important to George. You do not realize. He would not simply kill for her. He would die for her as well. He is in love.'

'Reid, what the shit are you playing at, man?'

'Monika. I'm going to kill that bitch. I don't know what she's at but she went too far this time. I'm going to kill her.'

'OK, so you got drunk and she dropped you somewhere. What did you do, try it on with her again? She's said no about a million times already, Reid.'

'Wrap it up, Peter.'

'Yeah, well cool it with my car, OK.'

Januz was in the back smoking a cigar and looking out of the window with a peaceful smile. His passivity annoyed Reid even more, but the Yugoslav let it wash over him. Reid had arrived in Harry Lime's, stinking of alcohol and stale urine, at eleven, shouting for Peter and cursing Monika. Januz had said to him that he should quieten down or leave, he was disturbing the other customers. Reid, recognizing the dangerous edge to Januz's tone, fell silent and walked to the back of the bar where Peter was talking with the barmaid. 'You,' he had said, 'let's go. Keys.' Peter had casually slung his jacket over his shoulder and led the way to the car, but Januz took the keys and refused to hand them over until Reid told them what had happened and where they were going. 'You see Monika?' Januz told him she had come by earlier. 'So why don't you know? I told her the address. She's probably gone there already, the bitch.' Januz had agreed that it was possible.

'I don't believe it. She is here. That's her VW.' Reid parked the Audi behind Adele's car and the three of them crossed the street to the front entrance. Before Reid could go through into the building, however, Januz grabbed him by the arm and pushed him against the wall, gripping the lapels of his jacket tightly.

'OK, friend. We're here. And we will find Adele and George and maybe Monika and they will not offer you a cup of tea when you go in there.'

'Let me go.'

'No. Not until you calm down again. Are you calm, Reid? Good. Now, I will lead the way and, when we see George, I will do the talking.'

Reid nodded and Januz slapped his cheek gently before leading them through into the courtyard.

'These stairs? They seem to go to the top. George told me it was in an attic.'

When they reached the apartment there was a light shining from inside but no sound could be heard. Januz tapped on the door. It creaked on its hinges slightly and Reid tried to push past.

'You will wait.'

He swung open the door and stepped inside, glancing at the Schiele on his left as he passed through to the studio bedroom. Reid stopped in front of the desk and stared at the painting.

'At bloody last. Would you believe it.'

'The real thing?'

Reid nodded, his mouth open in wonder as it all sank in.

'It's worth a fortune, Peter. Worth more exactly because it isn't signed. Look at that. Just the date. 1917. Perfect. Absolutely perfect.'

'So where's Adele and George? And Monika.'

Reid waved Peter through to the room where Januz had gone.

Januz was just inside the door studying the painting on Adele's easel. Only the faintest shadow of George's torso and limbs seemed to emerge from the neutral background, built up with clear glaze to give it texture and depth, though from other angles it would seem not to be there. And in vivid detail, splashed onto the canvas in the primary colours, were George's eyes, his lips, his hair and one hand which covered his genitals. Red lips, a red hand, blue eyes, yellow hair. Beneath Adele's signature was an inscription: 'Virtue dies but is born again, more exacting than ever.'

Peter read it aloud and Januz said: 'Camus. Of course. She was always quoting him to George, so he told me. They're dead, Peter. I covered them up. On the bed. They used morphine. From that old medicine cabinet.'

Peter walked over to the bed, pulled back the canvas-coloured sheet and looked at Adele and George lying in each other's arms, their eyes closed. George's expression was peaceful. It took Peter a moment to realize that it was Monika lying there with him. He drew back and turned to face Januz who said: 'Somehow it isn't a surprise.'

As Peter ran out of the room Reid came in, his mouth open in astonishment when he saw Adele's painting.

'I'll never be able to look at George in the same way again, you know. . . .'

Januz whipped round and punched him twice, once in the stomach and once in the face and, as Reid crumpled to the floor, he carefully picked Adele's painting from the easel before walking out of the apartment, down the iron staircase, across the courtyard and out of the building to the car where Peter was waiting for him.

'Come on, friend. I have a bar to run.'

'And a picture to hang.'

'Yes. And a picture to hang. And that.'